"Alex, I have something to tell you," she said.

"Your tone of voice worries me."

"It's nothing bad. It's about that 'virus' I was fighting in February." She took another deep breath. "Do you remember that big fight we had in January?"

"Yeah," he said, "I do. I can't remember what it was about, though."

"It doesn't matter now," she said. "What's important is how we made up the next day," she added.

She could feel him staring at her. Was he remembering that night? They'd made love with a vengeance, downstairs in front of a blazing fire, and had slept there all night. "I've been trying to tell you this since you got home," she added. "I was wrong about the cause of my nausea. Brace yourself. I'm about four months pregnant."

She could see the whites of his eyes widen. "Say that again," he whispered.

"We're going to have a baby."

STRANDED

ALICE SHARPE

This book is dedicated to sweet Ruby Rose.
Welcome, baby.

ISBN-13: 978-0-373-74828-0

STRANDED

This edition published by arrangement with Harlequin Books S.A.

For questions and comments about the quality of this book, please contact us at CustomerService@Harlequin.com.

Printed in U.S.A.

ABOUT THE AUTHOR

Alice Sharpe met her husband-to-be on a cold, foggy beach in Northern California. One year later they were married. Their union has survived the rearing of two children, a handful of earthquakes registering over 6.5, numerous cats and a few special dogs, the latest of which is a yellow Lab named Annie Rose. Alice and her husband now live in a small rural town in Oregon, where she devotes the majority of her time to pursuing her second love, writing.

Alice loves to hear from readers. You can write her c/o Harlequin Books, 233 Broadway, Suite 1001, New York, NY 10279. An SASE for reply is appreciated.

Books by Alice Sharpe

HARLEQUIN INTRIGUE

746—FOR THE SAKE OF THEIR BABY
823—UNDERCOVER BABIES
923—MY SISTER, MYSELF*
929—DUPLICATE DAUGHTER*
1022—ROYAL HEIR
1051—AVENGING ANGEL
1076—THE LAWMAN'S SECRET SON‡
1082—BODYGUARD FATHER‡
1124—MULTIPLES MYSTERY
1166—AGENT DADDY
1190—A BABY BETWEEN THEM
1209—THE BABY'S BODYGUARD
1304—WESTIN'S WYOMINGΔ
1309—WESTIN LEGACYΔ
1315—WESTIN FAMILY TIESΔ
1385—UNDERCOVER MEMORIES§
1392—MONTANA REFUGE§
1397—SOLDIER'S REDEMPTION§
1501—SHATTERED**
1507—STRANDED**

*Dead Ringer
‡Skye Brother Babies
ΔOpen Sky Ranch
§The Legacy
**The Rescuers

CAST OF CHARACTERS

Alex Foster—This police detective apparently fell off the face of the earth three months before. Now he learns his travails were no twist of fate, nor are they over. But someone isn't counting on Alex's fierce determination to rebuild his marriage and protect his wife at any cost to himself.

Jessica Foster—Alex's wife isn't sure how she feels about her marriage or which secrets to share with Alex. But she does know someone is out to wreak havoc on their lives. It's time to take a stand.

Nate Matthews—Alex's best friend from way back has struggled with the same issues facing Alex. He's managed to survive. His goal is to make sure Alex does the same.

Dylan Hobart—Alex's partner on the Blunt Falls Police Department is a bodybuilder with an eye for the fairer sex. It takes him a while to declare his intention to watch Alex's back but when he does, he makes it clear he'll see it through to the bitter end.

Billy Summers—Everyone agrees this handyman is a nice guy, and it's obvious he has something he wants to tell Alex. But, wow, he's sure having trouble saying it.

Lynda Summers—Billy's mother is the town's fallen beauty with so many problems it's hard to see where one stops and another begins. What is her hold on Chief Smyth? And exactly how many men are using her?

Chief Smyth—He's a tricky guy. Part publicity hound, part dedicated lawman, a family man with a dash of arrogance and a sprinkle of hostility. He's suspicious of almost everyone, especially Alex. Or is that an act?

Kit Anderson—This patrolman wants to be a detective, a goal that seemed attainable until Alex showed back up in Blunt Falls. How far will he go to make his dreams come true?

John Miter—He's just flat-out an enigma. How dangerous is he?

Tad and Ted Cummings—Are these attractive, personable twins really Billy's pals, or does the friendship have a darker side?

Charles Bond, aka William Turner—A shadowy figure everyone is looking for. His agenda includes murder and mayhem as vehicles to spread fear. Can he be stopped in time to avert a disaster?

Prologue

February

To Alex Foster, the flight between Blunt Falls, Montana, and Shatterhorn, Nevada, felt ill-fated from the get-go. The unexpected deteriorating weather was just the latest obstacle, but at least it was one that could be managed by some decent flying skills and a deviation from his flight plan.

He yawned and rubbed his eyes, fighting a growing fatigue he couldn't afford. Unscrewing the cap on a new bottle of the vitamin-enhanced water he carried when he piloted his plane, he took a long swallow. The numbers on the charts swam before his eyes and he blinked, performed a few fuzzy calculations and changed radio frequencies to the Bozeman, Montana beacon. He banked the plane toward the east, hoping to avoid the worst of the system and arrive just a little late.

No big deal. Nate would explain the facts of life when it came to flying to their friend Mike. And

Mike's issues would be there in two hours or two days—they weren't going away anytime soon. The poor guy had been devastated by the incident all three men shared last Labor Day when a lone teenage gunman had shot and killed four kids in a random attack at a Nevada shopping mall. Since then, Mike had been gathering data he believed hinted at a conspiracy. This meeting would let them review what Mike had learned and maybe, hopefully, help him get past some of his wild ideas.

A glimpse out the Cessna window revealed nothing but icy-white sky that seemed to swirl in his head. He climbed higher, hoping to find less turbulent air. He was kind of glad Jessica hadn't come along. She'd claimed she was fighting a virus and he'd accused her of making it up so she wouldn't have to be with him. Maybe some time apart would help, he didn't know. However, now, with his vision blurring and his stomach turning, he considered he might owe her an apology.

He yawned again and took another swallow of the drink as he tried to quench his thirst.

After thirty more minutes, the break in the weather he'd anticipated still hadn't materialized. His eyes drifted shut and he opened them quickly, making himself sit up straighter. As he did periodically, he glanced at the control panel. It took him a second to actually register what he saw.

The oil-pressure indicator showed a rapid decline toward the red zone. He stared at the gauge with disbelief, then tapped the glass. At that moment he became aware of a burning odor and peered out the window where he found oil flying over the coaming. Liquid drops hit the windshield and crawled away, leaving portentous snail-like tracks on the glass.

A quick check of the gauge showed pressure still falling. He flipped the radio frequencies again, but the unit was now silent. He tore off the headphones as flames flared from the engine compartment. Almost simultaneously, he pulled the handle to turn off the fuel tanks and yanked on the fire extinguisher lever. Smoke billowed from under the cowling, but dissipated at once.

And then the engine seized.

The fire was out but the plane was dead.

Disaster was imminent. He was off his flight plan, somewhere over the Bitterroot Mountains in the middle of the Rockies. He had an EPIRB aboard and knew the emergency beacon would signal once activated by a crash, but unlike the newer models that communicated with satellites, his older unit required a search plane to fly directly overhead. Would anyone look for him this far afield from his expected route?

The plane began losing altitude. He spiraled down through the clouds, into the storm. Visibility cleared for a few seconds and he saw a large snow-covered meadow to the north. He quickly corrected his course to aim for that, going into a glide, pushing the yoke ahead to avoid a stall.

Seconds seemed to drag and then everything sped up as the ground once again appeared closer than ever. The plane skimmed over the snowy treetops ringing the meadow and shuddered as it made its first bounce. That was immediately followed by the scream of twisted metal as the landing-gear struts tore from their housings. The wounded plane skimmed along the snow on its belly, racing into the middle of the meadow, snow flying at the windshield.

At last the Cessna came to an abrupt and sudden stop. Alex flew forward into the instrument panel. His chest impacted with the yoke, his left leg caught and twisted in the mangled metal below. The outside of the cabin was covered with snow. He wiped something from his eyes—blood—then immediately struggled with the door, pushing against the buildup, knowing he had to get it open before it froze shut. He almost choked on relief as weak daylight flooded the cabin.

A strange cracking noise drove ice picks through his nervous system. The noise came again and he recognized it for what it was. With horror, he looked down to find water rising over his shoes. As quick as he'd ever done anything in his life, he grabbed his backpack and the medical kit and threw both through the open door. He undid his seat belt, took a steadying breath and screamed with pain as he ruthlessly extricated his leg. There was blood everywhere but he'd have lots of time to worry about that later. If there was a later…

Clenching his teeth, he used his upper-body strength to pull himself through the open door.

This was no meadow; this was a lake covered with ice and the plane, heavy with unspent fuel, had broken through. He scrambled out the door and landed on his gear. The fall sent a stab of unbearable agony racing from his heel to his groin, and he had to struggle to keep from passing out. Priority one: keep himself and his gear from going into the water. Get away, get away, as fast as possible, beat the cracks spreading out around him. His hands were clumsy as he tied things together and then he dragged himself away from the wreck, using his elbows for traction, trailing his gear from his belt, the fissures continuing to open up all around him.

Chapter One

Three Months Later

Jessica's cell phone rang as she sat at her desk grading a math quiz. She jumped in her seat and swallowed a lump of panic as she dug the device from the jacket hanging over the back of her chair. You'd think after all this time a ringing phone wouldn't cause this fearful knee-jerk reaction, but it did and it probably always would. Until they found his body, anyway. Or until she knew the truth.

She clicked it on and said, "Yes?" in a breathless voice because she didn't recognize the number on the screen and that was always nerve-racking. How many times had she imagined learning news of Alex's fate from a stranger? Almost as many times as she'd imagined him calling her himself from some secret spot in Middle America where he'd gone to start a life without her. That was the trouble when a husband simply vanished.

You never knew if he was dead or alive; you lived in limbo. Any closure would be better than none.

The caller was a salesman wanting to know if she needed new drainpipes and she got rid of him right away. The truth was, her house was in limbo, too. If it wasn't for Billy Summers and his sweet-natured persistence in helping her with chores, she imagined she would just let the place crumble around her.

And that had to end. She had to get a grip. Maybe it was time to think about selling the house, getting something smaller. Could she do that? Not yet. But the question nagged her: What would she do if Alex walked through the door?

The sun beating through the high windows made the room too warm. She folded her arms on her desk and rested her forehead against her hands, closing her eyes. Restless nights usually caught up with her in the late afternoon, and apparently today was no exception. The school was mostly empty now, but occasional footsteps moving in the halls gave her a reassuring feeling of not being alone as did the faint whirring and beeping of distant machines set to automatic timers.

Thank goodness the school term was almost finished and she'd been allowed to back out of teaching summer school this year. She loved the kids in her remedial classes at Blunt Falls High, but she needed time away from them and everyone else. Who would have guessed constant pity could be so exhausting? She closed her eyes and let her mind drift for a while.

A nearby noise jerked her out of her stupor and she looked up to find a stranger standing in her open doorway. As the school was very strict about allowing unauthorized people on the campus, this man had to be someone's father, but he didn't look like any other parent she'd met at this school. He was tall and dark, thin, with uncut hair and a full beard. Dark glasses covered his eyes. His jeans and corduroy shirt appeared too big for his frame, while his face and hands were weathered looking. There was a healed abrasion across one cheekbone and another slashing across what she could see of his forehead. As he moved into the class, she detected a definite hitch in his left leg.

She found herself on her feet without consciously deciding to rise. "May I help you?"

He took off the dark glasses, folding them away as he continued moving between the desks. The look in his hazel eyes pinned her to the floor and she all but stopped breathing as her throat closed.

And then he was right beside her, taking her hands, looking at her as though he'd never seen her before. He brought her right hand up to his face and laid her palm against his hairy cheek. His eyes sparkled with tears.

"Alex?" she murmured, searching his face with a disbelieving intensity. "Oh, my God. Alex?"

His nod was almost imperceptible. His tears moistened her fingertips. "Are you real or am I dreaming?" she mumbled.

"If you're dreaming, then so am I," he said, his voice choked with emotion.

She forgot to wonder how she would feel or react and just flung herself against him. Tears of relief filled her eyes as he held her. She finally pushed herself away. "How is this possible?" she asked. "Where have you been?"

He pulled her back against him, burying his face against her neck, holding her tight as if he'd never let her go. "I crashed in the Bitterroots," he said. "I've just been trying to stay alive until the snow melted so I could get back."

"I thought you were dead," she said. "Or maybe even worse, that you..."

She stopped short.

"I can't believe I'm holding you," he whispered.

She leaned back to gaze up at him, smoothing his hair away from his brow with trembling fingers, trying to find the man she married under the scars and hair. "Are you all right? You're limping. And your poor face." She searched his eyes for answers.

Instead of providing them, he tugged her back to his chest, and this time his lips landed on hers.

Even when times were tough between them, the physical connection had been quicksilver and so it still was, all the sweeter for the fact that until a few minutes before, she'd thought she'd never see him again.

A woman's voice cut in from the open doorway and they both turned to find the school's principal, Silvia Greenspan. "I'm sorry to interrupt you guys," she said. It appeared she knew Alex was at the school, had probably spoken to him when he came onto the campus. She smiled at them both fondly as she added, "There are tons of reporters outside. Alex, I think someone in the office got excited and alerted the local television channel that you'd reappeared here at the school. I don't know how long we can hold them back." She turned and left, her footsteps clicking in retreat as she hurried back down the hall.

"How did you get to Blunt Falls?" Jessica asked.

"Doris and Duke Booker brought me. They're the people who more or less rescued me."

"Rescued you! Alex, what happened?"

"Later, okay?" He looked at her longingly. "There's so much I need to tell you."

"I know," she said, her mind still grappling with his offhand comment about being rescued. "Me, too."

"I'm sorry about the fight we had before I left. It was my fault."

"Not now," she said, straightening his collar. "You have to go talk to the press."

He shook his head. "No."

"What do you mean, no? Everyone is going to be so relieved to hear you're home safe and sound."

"They can wait," he said. He gestured at her cluttered desk. "Anything here need to go home with you?"

"These tests," she said, picking up the math papers she'd been grading. He retrieved her briefcase from the closet and held it open for her as she deposited the papers. "Why are we running away?"

"Because," he said, sounding like one of her students. "There's a back way out of here through the gym, isn't there?"

"Yes, but—"

"But nothing," he interrupted as he took her jacket from her chair and draped it over her shoulders. "Where's your purse?"

"I'll get it," she said as she unlocked the desk drawer where she kept it during classes. "Why don't you want to talk to the newspeople? What's wrong?"

"Nothing is wrong, not like that. I just think we have the right to reconnect before the blitz. Don't you?"

"Yes," she said, nodding, suddenly realizing he was right. There were so many things she had to tell him about the past three months, things he needed to understand, things that would redefine what he thought he knew about the world, things she didn't want him hearing from someone holding a camera on his face. And, she realized with a jolt of panic, there were things she needed to take care of, too. Things she didn't want him to see.

She followed him toward the door, his limp a visual reminder of the struggle he must have endured. "Hurry," she added as they raced down the hall and out the back of the gym toward the baseball field, which they could circle to access the parking lot.

It was a tremendous relief to slide behind the wheel of her car. "Duck your head," she muttered, driving out of the lot. Their path led them past two or three television vans with satellite dishes on their roofs and a growing crowd of people milling about. Alex didn't sit up again until they were half a mile away and she gave him the all clear. Their gazes met and he smiled but she knew it wouldn't be long before reporters figured out they'd slipped away.

And it wasn't as though they'd be hard to find.

"NOTHING MUCH HAS CHANGED," Alex said in wonder as he followed Jessica into the house and closed the front door behind them. It seemed surreal that for the past one hundred and three days he'd been living in the most primitive of conditions while his wife, his house, his job—his world—existed right here as it always had. At the time, emerged as he was in basic survival, all this had seemed like a distant fantasy he'd never live to revisit, but here it had been all along, chugging away without him, apparently none the worse for his absence.

The same thing had happened when he'd been deployed in the army, only then he'd been shot at, as well. On the other hand, he hadn't been alone and there was a lot to be said for companionship.

The house was a newer one, built in a cluster of similar houses located in a small wooded area a few miles outside of Blunt Falls. They'd bought it with plans to fill the rooms upstairs with their children and had pictured them running through the trees and splashing in the shallow stream at the bottom of the gulch with the neighborhood kids as playmates. But that had never happened. Oh, the neighbors' families grew all right, but theirs didn't and now, in some ways, the houses all around them, strewn with tricycles and sandboxes, formed a painful reminder that things didn't always work out the way you thought they would.

Now the house welcomed him back with years of memories, and he stood by the big rock fireplace just trying to center himself. Meanwhile, Jessica closed the drapes and turned to face him. She'd deposited her purse and briefcase on the chair nearest the door, much as she always had and now stood looking up the stairs as though she wanted to dash up to their room.

He reached for her hand. “We won’t have long before they track us down,” he said.

She looked at him and nodded. “Good point.”

“I’m a little beat,” he said with a smile. “Let’s go sit at the table like we used to. Let’s talk.”

“Yes,” she said, nodding. “Okay.”

He claimed the chair facing the living-room door and patted the one beside it. She entered the dining room behind him, her brown eyes velvety, enhanced by the oversize cream tunic she wore over slim black jeans.

She looked good, her auburn hair longer than it had been in a while, combed straight back from her oval-shaped face which was devoid of makeup as it almost always was. He’d been afraid he’d find her worn-out and grief stricken, but instead she seemed almost luminescent. His disappearance didn’t seem to have hurt her.

Well, why should it have? They’d been whisper close to a separation for most of the past year, so caught up in their different lives that they’d become like that old saying, “Ships passing in the night.” In fact, for the past three months his greatest fear had been that she would be relieved he’d vanished. No more fights, no more disappointments, no stress. Just over. And who was to say that that isn't what happened? Maybe she'd moved on, maybe she'd even found someone else.

Maybe he should stop borrowing trouble....

"Are you hungry?" she asked, standing behind the chair he'd patted. It provided a good view of the garden and he'd already noticed the plethora of bushes and flowers that bloomed with an intensity he didn't remember ever seeing before. Some plants were absolutely covered with buds, promising radiant blossoms in the weeks to come. She must have spent hours out there tending that garden, loving it.

"The Bookers stuffed me," he said, a bit distracted by the beauty sweeping across the yard toward the doors. He pulled his attention back to her. "They grow or hunt just about everything they eat. My poor digestive tract is probably struggling to cope after existing on three-plus months of pretty much nothing but fish."

She slid a basket of clothes across the table and started folding them. He got the distinct impression she was keeping her hands busy. Either that, or she was creating a barrier by positioning the basket between them. "Where did you meet these people?" she asked.

"I literally stumbled into their garden and collapsed in their asparagus patch."

She stopped folding a lacy bra and stared at him. He tore his gaze away from the undergarment and all the memories it provoked as she said, "You're not making any sense. Where have you been for three months? What exactly happened to you?"

He told her about the storm and the dead engine, ending with the crash far off his reported route and the immediate sinking of the plane. He touched on his nightmare crawl across the lake to the relative safety of the shore and how he'd managed to live through the first night by digging out a trench around the base of a tree and covering it over with evergreen boughs.

"I can't believe you survived," she said when he paused. "Did you ever see a search plane?"

"Once," he said, all but wincing at the memory. "I woke up to the sound of an engine and scrambled out of my hole like a crippled badger."

"When was this?"

"Two days after the crash. I had to grab the makeshift crutches to get out into the clear where they could see me. The emergency beacon I carried went down with the Cessna."

She almost rolled her eyes and he smiled. "I know, I know. You asked me to update my equipment a hundred times."

"Two hundred," she said.

"Well, you were obviously right. Anyway, by the time I got out from under the trees, they were gone and they didn't come back."

"That must have been horrible," she said, visibly shuddering. "How is your leg now?"

"Pretty good. I'll probably limp for the rest of my life, but considering everything, that's not so bad."

She nodded. "Okay, now tell me how you ended up in an asparagus patch."

He shrugged as though it was all no big deal. The actuality of it was a whole different matter. "I waited until the snow started to melt, smoked a bunch of fish, broke camp and stared downhill, following a stream that fed from the lake. After a few days, I ran into tended land, though I didn't see a house. There was this big, tall fence surrounding some seedlings so I went through the gate to see if anything was mature enough to eat yet. I found a few strawberries, gobbled them up and must have passed out or fallen asleep because the next thing I knew, an older woman was shaking me awake. She told me her name was Doris and that she and her husband, Duke, had built themselves a place just over the rise. They nursed me for a day or so and then they insisted on driving me home and that took another two days."

"Thank heavens she found you," Jessica said. "You should see a doctor about your leg."

"I will. Right now, it's enough just to be sitting here." He ran a hand across his hairy chin and added, "I need a shave and my own clothes. Duke lent me these."

"They sound like incredibly kind people. But, Alex, why didn't you phone me?"

"They don't have a phone," he said. "No television, no internet, no electricity. They're the back-to-nature type. I did call my parents on the way, though."

"But not me."

Did that bother her? Was she thinking that in the months before he disappeared he'd often not reported in as often as he should because it always seemed to come with an argument or apathy, either one of them hard to take? "I didn't want you to find out about me over a phone," he said gently. "I wanted to see you. I wanted to look in your eyes, to know if it mattered to you that I was alive."

"Of course it matters to me," she said, brow furling. "What a terrible thing to say."

"You know what I mean, Jess."

She nodded as she bit her lip and took a deep breath.

"Still," he continued, gesturing at the wall phone. "I'm kind of surprised that thing isn't ringing off the hook. Mom has had time to tell all the relatives by now."

"I have it switched to message only," she said. "I had to. It felt like every call was a possible ambush. I had to be able to deal with people on my own terms, at least once I was inside this house." She met his gaze and smoothed back her hair. "I'm sorry, Alex, that must sound selfish to you."

"No," he said gently, patting the chair again as she finished folding the laundry. "No, it sounds like survival, that's all."

She sat down next to him, their knees all but touching. He ached to fold her in his arms. He wanted to tell her that he'd been thinking of little else but her for weeks and weeks and that he wanted them to be together, to make things work. But she was distant and jittery and he wasn't brave enough to admit his feelings and have them dashed in his face.

For that matter, dare he trust his feelings? The past several days had been a roller coaster of a ride, exhausting on all levels. Being back was strange and wonderful and truth be known, scary as hell.

He caught her studying his face and wished he'd taken Duke Booker up on his offer for a shave and a haircut so he'd look a little more like he had before.

"There are things you need to know," she said.

He braced himself. Here it came. She'd moved on.

She shook her head as she added, "Maybe you should call Nate and get him to tell you."

"Nate?" What did his best friend have to do with her?

"He's been so concerned about you," she said.

"I can imagine," Alex murmured, trying to imagine what it must have been like for Nate to keep waiting for a plane that never arrived. They'd met in the army, had both ended up with careers in law enforcement, Nate as a deputy in Arizona and Alex a police detective in Blunt Falls. Now they were fishing buddies when the opportunity allowed.

"What does Nate need to tell me that you can't?" he asked.

She shook her head. "Okay, I'll try to explain. Before people start asking you questions, you've got to know a few things. There are a lot of people, Nate included, who don't think your plane crash was an accident."

He frowned. "What?"

"Right around the time your plane disappeared, Nate was almost killed. That's why he couldn't join the search to try to find you. Worse than all that, though, is that Mike Donovan was murdered."

"Mike is dead?"

"Yes. I'm sorry."

Mike wasn't a close pal, like Nate, but Alex had cared for him all the same. Head spinning, he murmured, "Nate thinks all three of us were targeted by the same person?"

"Yes, a man in Shatterhorn who sang your accolades after the mall incident. Everyone refers to him simply as The Shatterhorn Killer and not by name, a tribute to those he killed or caused to die. Anyway, he's dead now, thanks to an unidentified driver Nate saw purposefully run him down with a car. This same man was also behind the shooting at the Shatterhorn mall and apparently, him and others like him have been responsible for all sorts of mayhem occurring on national holidays around the country. Remember that incident in Hawaii last Pearl Harbor Day where some angry kid shot and killed those off-duty soldiers on the beach? Things like that. Everyday events shattered by violence. And everyone is certain something is going to happen this Memorial Day, too."

Alex stared at her a moment, trying to make sense of all this. "But you said the guy was run over."

"There are apparently others. Even if this man wasn't in Blunt Falls when your plane was sabotaged, he could have hired someone to help him do it."

Alex simply couldn't wrap his head around any of it. The lonely austerity of the mountains suddenly seemed like the epicenter of civilization and this place a jungle. "Why would anyone do this?" he asked.

"Oh, it's complicated, Alex. Something about creating terror for people engaged in normal, ordinary situations so they won't support any kind of weapon control. It's domestic terrorism but with a spin. They call themselves patriots and they recruit malcontent kids to do the dirty work. It's been in the news lately, but I've been a little distracted.... Nate can tell you more and I know the FBI and FAA are going to want to talk to you, too."

Welcome home, he thought. Here all this time he'd assumed he'd been in an everyday kind of plane crash, no intrigue, no drama, just rotten luck and maybe a bad gasket or something. And now he was hearing someone may have tried to murder him.

The fact was the day of the crash was something of a blur. He hadn't felt very good; he'd thought he was getting Jessica's flu. He'd been tired and thirsty and out of it, and then the plunging oil pressure, so sudden and dramatic and final.

Could that have been caused by someone tampering with his plane? But he'd had the required maintenance performed on the plane—in fact, he was a stickler for that. He'd also conducted a preflight check. He could vaguely remember doing it although like everything else about that day, the recollection was hazy.

"We don't know for sure that your crash was premeditated, but it's awfully coincidental," Jessica said, and he wasn't positive but it sounded to him as though she was trying to ease some of his shock.

"Yeah," he said. He took a deep breath before trying to shy away from all of this for a moment. "How about you?" he asked. "How have you been? Did anyone try to harm you?"

"No, I've been fine," she said, and then shook her head. "That's not true. I've been a wreck."

"In some odd way, I'm glad to hear it," he admitted. He took a deep breath. "I've had all sorts of time to regret what I said that last morning. I shouldn't have even suggested you were lying to me about having the flu."

"I wasn't making it up, you know. I really did feel sick."

"I know. I think I had a touch of it, too. It's just that we'd been going our own ways so often that it was beginning to feel like we'd never hook back up."

"I know," she said.

"You began to say something earlier," he added. "Something like, there being something worse than me being dead. You stopped yourself. What were you going to say? What would have been worse than me being dead?"

She blinked a few times and he could almost see

the wheels turning in her head. "I don't remember where I was going with that," she said at last.

Their gazes met and she looked away. She may not have been lying about having a virus but she was lying now, he was sure of it. He wanted to demand she explain, but he couldn't bring himself to further distance her. The warmth they'd shared in her classroom had evaporated as soon as they hit the house. How ironic would it be to survive what he'd survived just to lose everything that really mattered?

But had he really thought he could waltz back in here and erase the past year or two of tension between them with a few kisses and an apology?

"We can try again," he said very softly, searching her face.

"Try again? What do you mean?" she asked.

"Having a baby. I know you said before that you were finished hoping but I've been thinking about that, too. The doctor might have been wrong. We could consult another specialist."

"Please, Alex," she said, staring into his eyes. "This is all too much. An hour ago I thought I'd never see you again. There are things we need to discuss." She smiled and added, "That's a real understatement."

There was a sudden knock on the front door and they both turned their heads and stared into the living room as though expecting an invasion.

"I think our time before the blitz is about up," he said as the doorbell chimed. He could hear voices coming from outside and more knocks seemed to rattle the windows. "Continue with what you were saying," he urged.

"Not now, not like this," she said with a shake of her head. She pushed a few strands of hair away from her face and smiled. "Later, okay? I'll go stick these clothes in the bedroom. Will you answer the door?"

"Might as well get it over with," he said as he got to his feet. But for a second he stood there watching Jessica hurry into the kitchen with the basket on her hip. He knew she would take the back stairs up to their bedroom.

What he didn't know was what she was trying to tell him.

Chapter Two

Jessica's laptop sat on her desk. With barely a pause, she set the laundry basket aside and opened the computer. Within a few seconds, she was at her Facebook page where she spent several minutes deleting a post she'd made almost two months earlier and which she hoped and prayed Alex would never know existed.

What she'd written had seemed reasonable at the time, like turning over every rock, but now in light of what she knew, it seemed the very essence of double-crossing on her part.

She deleted all pertinent comments from friends and family and closed the laptop, able to really take a breath for the first time in an hour. Then she moved to the window and pulled aside the drape. From this vantage point, she could see all the media trucks parked outside. Several neighbors had wandered over, apparently curious about what was going on. Alex, a lone, weathered-looking figure, stood on the front lawn facing the crowd, his back to Jessica. After months of solitude, what must this day be like for him?

She hurried down the stairs, pausing to take a deep breath before going outside. They'd been a team once upon a time, like right after their marriage when no life-altering disappointments had pushed them apart. Could they be a team again?

Well, one thing was for sure. There was far too much at stake not to at least try. It was time to join Alex.

She stood to the side as he skirted questions, explaining how he'd survived and how he'd finally been able to get home. But reporters asking him about his plane and what went wrong got vague answers and he flatly refused to comment on the possibility of sabotage. He said it was too soon to talk like that, he needed more information.

Jessica was proud of the way he handled himself but not surprised. He could be a very articulate and commanding man when he wanted to be. Those qualities had drawn her to him in the first place and as she listened to him now, she once again wondered how they had grown so far apart.

When he saw her standing near, he extended his arm to welcome her to stand beside him and she did. Flashbulbs popped at the reunited, happy couple and she smiled as best she could.

Much later that night, she woke up in the middle of a dream whose details vanished upon opening her eyes. She reached across the sheets as she had done so many times before, knowing this time, finally, she would find Alex. When her fingers met nothing but rumpled sheets and blanket, she sat up and switched on the light.

For one blinding moment, she thought she'd dreamed Alex coming home. No, there on the chair was the corduroy shirt he'd borrowed from Duke Booker.

She got out of bed and shrugged on her robe, then went looking for him. The house was dark and silent and though she switched on enough lights to see where she was going, she couldn't find him anywhere. The garage still held his truck, which had been sitting in the same spot since she'd reclaimed it from the airport parking lot a few days after he vanished. That left only one place she could think of.

She didn't turn on the outside light. Closing the glass patio door behind her, she called his name into the dark and he responded at once. "Over here," he said, his voice coming from way back in the yard where it was deeply shadowed despite the moon overhead. However, she'd spent the past several restless weeks wandering around the garden at all times of the day and night and had no trouble finding her way.

Moonlight shone off the white roses that had just started to bloom. Some of the lilacs were still in flower, as well, and they added a deep, rich perfume to the night air.

Even though it was late May, temperatures dropped at night in Blunt Falls, and Jessica shivered in her thin robe. She used his voice as a guide until her vision adjusted to the dark, and then she could see him sitting on the rock wall that surrounded the pond where every spring, mallards raised their families.

"What are you doing out here at 3:00 a.m.?" she asked, but she knew. All evening she'd watched him pace the living room, turning away from his image on the television news, perusing the bookcase without touching a book, staring out the windows like a trapped animal. He'd taken a long walk after a supper he barely touched and, though he hadn't asked her not to come, she could tell he wanted to be alone. She'd determined to come clean with him right after the news conference, but his remote demeanor had kept her lips sealed.

She knew all the revelations she'd had to tell him in such a hurry weighed heavily on his mind, especially when he hadn't been able to reach Nate. But what else could she do? He had to know what had happened in his absence and it wasn't as if the rest of the world would give him a chance to recover from his ordeal before telling him all the gory details. After switching the phone back on, their evening had consisted of one call after the other until they finally turned it off again.

She'd gone to bed before him, worn-out from the day and exhausted trying to figure out where they went from here. He'd changed so much over the years and the horrible thing was that she wasn't sure exactly when it had happened. It was easy to blame their problems on not being able to have a child, but plenty of marriages thrived through much worse.

She knew things had gone downhill after the mall shooting in Shatterhorn where he and Nate had been involved in trying to stop a teenage gunman. He'd come home shaken to the core but he wouldn't talk to her about it. She'd seen the pictures in the newspaper, though—the broken glass, the blood spatters, the candlelight vigils.... No one came away from something like that without scars. But it had hurt her that he couldn't trust her with his feelings. Impatient with him, she'd allowed him to retreat even further into his work and his world.

But maybe it was even before that, even before the fertility doctors had told them to set their sights on something besides a big family unless they were open to adoption. Alex had refused to even entertain the thought of adoption and that had cut her as deep as her body's inability to conceive a child.

With nothing to say to one another and with each nursing their own disappointments, it had been easier to let go than hold on. There had been times while he was missing that she felt almost at peace with things and that now shamed her down to her toes.

"I couldn't sleep," he said softly.

She sat down on the rocks beside him, brushing aside the tulips and the forsythia. "It's hard being back, isn't it?"

He laughed under his breath. "It's all I wanted for months, to escape the snow and the outdoors and quiet—things I now miss in some ways." He put his hand over hers. "But don't think I'd rather be there than here. You know that, right?"

"Right," she said softly.

"We'll work things out," he said as if he'd been thinking about the same things she'd been thinking about.

"I hope we can," she said.

There was a moment of silence as they both folded their hands in their own laps and stared into the night. "You've really kept the yard up nice," he finally said.

"You can see it in the dark?" she teased.

"Almost. It seems to glow. But really, I noticed it earlier today. I've never seen anything like it. How did you manage it all by yourself?

"I didn't," she admitted. "Do you remember Billy Summers?"

"The kid who does odd jobs at the airfield? What about him?"

"After you…didn't come home…he showed up on the doorstep. I hadn't seen him since he graduated from high school and that has to be at least three years ago now. He'd heard about your plane disappearing and he wanted to know if he could help me. I refused at first, but he kept coming back and offering. I started giving him odd jobs. He proved to be very reliable, especially when it came to the yard."

"I would never have guessed that of Billy Summers."

"I know. He was a surprise. I told him about how I always bought flowers for the veterans' graves on Memorial Day and he offered to plant some if I would tell him how. He brought me some little index cards and I wrote the directions down for him in simple words. I saw him checking the instructions all the time, but I don't really think they were necessary. He seems to have a way with plants. Anyway, we owe the flowers to Billy."

"And we'll be able to skip the last-minute dash to the big-box store to order flowers for Memorial Day," Alex said.

She nodded and bit her lip. She'd been about to tell Alex that all last week she'd planned to honor his memory and years of service, as well. He didn't need to hear that. "Alex, I have something to tell you," she said.

"Your tone of voice worries me."

"It's nothing bad. It's about that 'virus' I was fighting in February." She took another deep breath. "Do you remember that big fight we had in January?"

"Yeah," he said, "I do. I can't remember what it was about, though."

"It doesn't matter now," she said, but she could have enlightened him. He'd been working extra shifts, coming home late and grumpy. Talk about water under the bridge. "What's important is how we made up the next day," she added.

She could feel him staring at her. Was he remembering that night? They'd made love with a vengeance, downstairs in front of a blazing fire and slept there all night. "I've been trying to tell you this since you got home," she said. "I was wrong about the cause of my nausea. Brace yourself. I'm about four months pregnant."

She could see the whites of his eyes widen. "Say that again," he whispered.

"We're going to have a baby," she said, wishing she had waited until morning to tell him so she could see the expression on his face.

"I can't believe this," he said, springing to his

feet. "Four months? Are you okay, shouldn't you be lying down or something?"

"No. The doctor said if it's going to stick, it's going to stick."

"You shouldn't be working every day, should you?" he asked, and she could hear the panic in his voice. She understood how he felt, how amazing this must seem to him. It was the same to her, the difference being that she'd had months to get used to the idea, she'd spoken to the doctor, she knew what was going on.

"Summer vacation is coming and then the baby is due in October and with you home, I won't go back to work right away. Really, Alex, everything is fine. What I wanted to explain is that I found out about it a week or two after you disappeared. And that's why I got on Facebook. See—"

He interrupted her by pulling her to her feet and crushing her in his arms. "This is absolutely wonderful! I can hardly believe it. I promise you I'll do everything I can to make you happy. I love you."

She closed her eyes and held on to him. In a way, it was like he'd finally come home.

AFTER LAYING AWAKE for what seemed like hours, Alex got up quietly the next morning. He'd been rising with the sun and it felt unnatural to lie there when he could see daylight filtering through the curtains.

Besides, there was a lot on his mind.

Mentally he made a list. Call Nate. Make sure he still had a job on the Blunt Falls police force. Get checked out by the doctor.

He looked down at Jessica's slumbering face and added the most important thing of all: win back his wife before his baby was born.

She was so beautiful with her hair spilling over her pillow like a billowing russet-colored cloud, her lashes sweeping her cheeks, her peachy lips soft and yielding. No wonder she glowed. She was having a baby, his baby, after eight years of trying. He knew what it meant to her, he knew what it meant to him. And the urge to protect her at all costs surged through his body.

He had to pull himself together. Just as he'd planned for and worked toward walking out of the mountains every single day of his exile, he now had to put that behind him and work at moving forward in his marriage, in his job, in his life. What's done was done. He couldn't erase the past, but he could learn from it.

His reflection in the mirror wasn't particularly inspiring. The healed gashes across his cheek and forehead caused by the Cessna's broken windshield hadn't healed perfectly. But inside he knew he was stronger and more focused than he'd ever been and it was time to put all that energy to work.

The first thing he did was call Nate in Arizona.

Again. The phone switched immediately to message and he wasn't sure if there was any point in leaving one. Nate had a habit of disappearing into the wild with his horse and a dog or two for days on end, fishing and camping, no phone, no interruptions.

On the other hand, Alex knew his best friend would appreciate knowing he was back from the dead, so he left a message. Then he went downstairs to start a pot of coffee for Jessica, something he'd dreamed about doing over and over again, only this time it was for real. He found the bag of coffee beans where they'd always been, but they were labeled as decaf, he supposed in deference to her pregnancy. Still, the freshly ground beans smelled like heaven on earth and even the familiar perking sounds were like music. He didn't like to drink the stuff, but he used to make her a cup and carry it upstairs to her bed every morning when they were first married. He wasn't sure when that had stopped.

For himself, he dared hope he might find one of his favorite drinks in the back of the fridge where he left it months ago. Unless Jessica had thrown it out, of course. He opened the refrigerator quickly, wondering how long it would be before things like electricity would stop amazing him, dug behind a giant jar of pickles and came up with an icy bottle of Vita-Drink.

Happy days. It tasted great.

A light rapping on the glass kitchen door finally got through to him. Only friends and family came around the back like this and he braced himself for another homecoming as he went to see who it was.

He opened the door when he saw his partner on the police force, Detective Dylan Hobart. At the sight of Alex, Dylan's rugged face split into a giant grin. He wasn't wearing his usual jeans and T-shirt covered with an old military-looking vest adorned with patches and badges he'd earned as a former marine. Instead he wore a tight T-shirt and a leather jacket that fit him like a glove. He might be approaching forty-five, but he wasn't going without a struggle.

"If you aren't a sight for sore eyes," Dylan cried as he wrapped Alex in a one-armed bear hug. Then he pushed him away and stared at his face. "Holy cow, what happened to you? Damn, man, you've lost weight!"

Alex laughed. "You try eating nothing but fish for three months straight and see if you maintain all that mass." Dylan lived and breathed to lift weights and work out and he had the physique to prove it.

Dylan now produced the morning newspaper from where he'd apparently folded it into his rear pocket. "You're all over the place, man," he said, tapping the newsprint where Alex glimpsed a picture of himself and Jessica standing on the front lawn. He'd still had the beard when the picture was taken though he'd shaved it off later last night. He touched his smooth jaw and felt a little naked.

"I tried calling," Dylan said, "and then I thought, what the hell, I'm going over there and see that loser with my own eyes. I can't believe you walked out of those mountains. Are you really okay?"

Alex assured him he was fine. But Dylan's next question was more difficult to answer.

"What happened? I mean, I imagine you are sick to death of being asked this question, but did you drive your plane into a mountain or something? The article didn't really say."

"I made some coffee for Jess," Alex said, pouring his partner a mug. "Warning—it's decaf." They sat opposite each other at the counter. Alex drank the last of his water, and sighed. "I'm not sure what happened," he said.

"What do you mean?"

"A lot went down all at once. The oil leaked out of the engine somehow and then the engine froze and I'd been flying all over hell and breakfast trying to skirt a weather front. I landed on a lake and the plane sank. I was hurt, and so that confused the issue, too. Pretty much end of story."

"Pretty much beginning of story you mean," Dylan said with a knowing look in his light blue eyes.

"Whatever, the point is I survived."

"Have you spoken with the FAA about it? Given what happened to your buddies in Shatterhorn, we had our share of speculation around here after you went missing. There were some who thought your plane was rigged to crash. It seems kind of far-fetched to me, though."

"I just don't know," Alex said. "I made a few calls last night. Someone named Struthers from the FBI is coming today. I'll listen to what he has to say."

"Well," Dylan added, "I guess the important thing is you're home."

"No kidding," Alex said with feeling. "Especially now. I found out last night that Jess is going to have a baby."

Dylan's lips curled into a smile. "That's great news. Are you and she…well, I know things were rocky—"

"We're going to work things out," Alex said with no equivocation in his voice. He would do what he had to do. He would figure out how to show Jessica she was the center of his universe.

"That's great. You're going to be a daddy! That must be why she posted that comment on Facebook. I wondered. Wow, man, she must be so excited."

"We both are," Alex said, then asked, "What comment?" Hadn't she mentioned something about Facebook the night before?

"She didn't tell you?" He took out his phone and spent a minute getting to the site he wanted. "This is her page, but the comment is gone."

"What did it say?" Alex asked.

"No big deal. Just asked you to contact her if you could."

"What?"

"It just said that if you were reading what she'd written, would you contact her because there was something important you needed to know. It must have been the baby, don't you think?"

Alex nodded as he adjusted his expression to hide how shocked he was by this revelation. Was that what she'd meant when she told him that she'd thought he was something worse than dead? That he was what—hiding? Did she really think he would run out on her like a coward?

"They didn't replace you at work," Dylan said as though unaware of the bomb he'd just detonated in Alex's gut. "It's been slow, so it's been fine, but lately things are picking up a little. You know, the weather warms up and all the crazies come out. There was talk they were going to promote Kit Anderson but they haven't done it yet. Chief Quill quit right after you disappeared when he was caught taking bribes. The mayor appointed Frank Smyth to fill the position until he makes a permanent decision. As far as I know, they've got you on the books as being on some kind of emergency leave."

Alex made himself concentrate on the conversation. "I'm surprised the mayor chose Frank instead of you to act as chief."

"Yeah, I was, too. But Frank likes the business end of things and getting his picture in the paper, you know what he's like. He probably sweet-talked the mayor and that's nothing I would do unless he was twenty, gorgeous and a she."

Alex nodded. He didn't know Frank all that well even though they'd worked side by side on occasion. Frankly, the new chief was something of an enigma to Alex. Touchy on one hand, egotistical on the other, never shy about tooting his own horn. It was hard to imagine him as the chief. On the other hand, Alex was grateful the guy had held open his job.

"You're probably going to break Kit's heart but he'll live through it," Dylan said. "I don't care how many classes he's been taking, I don't think he could pass the detective test, anyway."

They both turned as Jessica entered the kitchen. She'd wrapped a kimono around herself and Alex's gaze immediately dropped to her midsection where he tried to discern a bulge. She smiled at him and his gaze flew to her face. "It doesn't show too much yet," she said.

He tried out a smile and wished they were alone so he could ask her about the Facebook thing.

"Morning, Dylan," she said as she poured herself a cup of coffee. "It's good to see you."

"Sorry to barge in so early. I just had to look at this guy with my own eyes," he said. "I swear, I hate to say it, but I never thought I'd see him again."

"It's hard to believe he's home," she said.

Dylan turned back to Alex. "It says in the newspaper that you hurt your leg."

"No big deal," Alex said. "Besides, Jess has already heard all the gory details. Let's not bore her with more."

"Come off it," she protested. "You've barely told me anything."

"And that's because you have more important things to think about," he said as he got up from his stool and offered it to her. He suddenly realized he hadn't delivered her coffee because he let himself get sidetracked by Dylan. Oh, well, there was always tomorrow.

"More important than your survival? I don't think so," she said.

"The fact is I did survive. Hey, here's some good news. Dylan says my job is still open."

She shook her head as she glanced at Dylan. "He's in protective mode," she said. "I may not survive it."

"I'm not worried," Dylan said. "We spend a lot of time driving around together. I'll get sick of his stories by the end."

"That's true, you will," Alex said. The phone rang and he added, "I have a feeling that's Nate calling me back. I need to talk to him and it might take a while. Later, okay?"

"Sure," Dylan said as Alex sprinted off to grab the phone before the answering machine came on.

"I'D BETTER BE on my way," Dylan said. But he paused with his hand on the knob and looked back at Jessica. "I'm so glad things are finally working out for you two."

Dylan was such a strong, physically honed individual that there were times Jessica found being in the same room with him a little overwhelming. She knew he was divorced, liked fast cars and dated a lot of younger women but never the same one for very long. It always seemed his romances started out hot and heavy and then tapered off.

"I know you've had a rough time the last year or so," he added.

She really did not want to talk about her relationship with her husband, at least not with Dylan, so she smiled brightly. "That's all behind us now," she said.

He cocked his eyebrows as though he thought she was being very naive. Exactly what had Alex told him? Whatever it was, she didn't want to know, but she could imagine. Hadn't she discussed her struggling marriage with her girlfriends? There was no reason Alex shouldn't have done the same. "Do you work tonight?" she asked.

"Not unless something terrible happens," he said. "Knock on wood."

"Then why don't you come back around six o'clock. Bring along anyone from the office who's free. We'll have a little surprise party for Alex."

"Do you think he'll like that?" Dylan said.

"I think it might be easier for him to see people in an informal situation. He can bring everyone up to speed at the same time and not have to keep going over things."

"That sounds reasonable," Dylan said. "Why don't you make it potluck. I'll bring one of those veggie trays."

"Okay. Tell everyone to park around the block and come in the back way through the garden."

"You got it."

After he left, she went in search of Alex. She found he'd closed himself in the den and what she could hear of his voice sounded low and guarded.

A few minutes later, he emerged from the den and seemed surprised to find her standing there.

"I take it that was Nate?" she said.

"Yeah."

"I bet he's relieved to hear you're okay."

He put his arm around her and kissed the top of her head. "Yeah, of course."

"Did he explain things better than I did?" she asked as they started back toward the kitchen.

"He just gave me a few more facts. He talked about the B-Strong organization which was used as a front, stuff like that. And he says the authorities can't place the guy who killed Mike as being in Blunt Falls last February."

"Which means he must have had an accomplice here," she said.

"Exactly. Nate says the FBI hasn't found anyone, though. Oh, you'll be relieved to hear the concern about a Memorial Day attack seems to be centered on Seattle, Washington, not here."

"I'm not relieved about anything," she said stubbornly.

He stared into her eyes. "Nate has had a hard time. That shooting at the mall really gutted him. He thought he should be able to save those kids… and then he was injured and in the hospital. The authorities are going to be hell-bent on finding out if my plane was sabotaged but even if it was, it doesn't seem to me that it has a whole lot of bearing on the here and now."

"But we don't know that," she said. She bit her lip and added, "I get the feeling you're giving me the kid-glove treatment," she said. "I can be pregnant and concerned about other things at the same time, you know. I'm pretty good at multitasking."

"I don't want to argue with you," he said. "Just let me take care of this and you take care of our baby."

"Listen carefully," she said, her voice soft. "We drifted apart before, partly because our dreams of having children weren't coming true. Now they are, but you're using him or her as an excuse to push me away again. I don't want to live like that, Alex. You have to let me share your life."

"I know," he said. "That goes two ways."

"What does that mean?"

"It means you have to let me share yours, too."

"I'm not the one refusing to talk about things," she said defiantly.

He stared into her eyes and she had the feeling there was something he wanted to say. But he shook his head. He didn't say it but it was as clear as day. He didn't want to fight, he didn't want to risk alienating her, but that's exactly what he was doing.

She needed to think. "Are you hungry?" she asked him. "Would you like an omelet?"

"Sure. And maybe I could take you to dinner tonight so you don't have to cook."

"Let's just stay in," she said.

"Just the two of us," he said. "Sounds cozy."

Chapter Three

An hour later Alex came into the kitchen from the backyard where he'd been fixing a broken screen. As he paused to grab another Vita-Drink, he heard voices coming from the living room. A second after that, Jessica called his name.

A tall man with light brown skin and close-cut black hair stood in the living room beside her. He wore a very tailored dark suit accented with an equally sober steel-gray tie. His hand clutched the handle of a briefcase and to Alex's eyes, he had Federal Agent written all over him.

"Alex, this is Agent Struthers," Jessica said.

Alex offered his hand. They adjourned to the den where Alex once again told his story about the crash and walking out of the mountains. And once again, he had to face the fact that his memory of the minutes preceding the actual impact were hazy.

"I don't know if the plane was sabotaged," he finished. "I don't see how it could have been. I plan on visiting the mechanic out at the field to ask him if he has any ideas."

The agent, who had seated himself across the desk, thumbed through his notes. "You're talking about Anthony Machi of High Mountain Aviation and Maintenance?"

"Yes."

"The FAA, Homeland Security, the Transportation Department as well the FBI also spoke with Mr. Machi. Without any details of what actually occurred, he was unable to do more than speculate, of course. Now about the plane. It's totally submerged?"

"Yes. Nate Matthews is a deputy in Arizona and a friend of mine. He suggests we fly back to the lake and dive on the wreck. We're both certified and Nate's Arizona fishing buddy is a diver with the FAA."

"The FAA will raise the plane. You should get in touch with them before you do anything yourself," the agent said. "You'll need to pinpoint the exact location on one of their aerial maps."

"I already called them this morning. I'll go by later today," Alex said as he slid a look over at Jessica. She was doing exactly what he knew she'd be doing: glowering. "I was going to tell you all this," he said to her.

She looked away from him.

"There's one more thing we need to discuss,"

the agent said as he opened a different folder and perused the information inside. "First of all, you know about Mike Donovan's notebook, right? The one your friend Nate Matthews found?"

"Yes," Alex said. "Nate told me Mike kept the notebook to catalog his investigation into who was really behind the mall shooting. That's why we were getting together that weekend. Mike thought he was on the trail of a conspiracy."

"Yes," Struthers agreed. "And as it turns out, he was absolutely right. Mr. Donovan had written 'Seattle' on one of the pages along with the name of the man who appeared to head the B-Strong group that supposedly ran programs for strengthening young men's characters. There was also a date that happens to correspond to this coming Memorial Day. The current thinking is that something the Shatterhorn Killer set in motion is going to occur in Seattle in a few short days."

"But the Shatterhorn Killer is dead," Alex said.

Struthers nodded. "Which brings me to a recent development. As part of our investigation, we're running a wiretap on a suspect phone in Seattle. I was contacted because this person received a call from a former employee of the Shatterhorn Killer. There was mention of a contact in Blunt Falls which is why it was called to my attention. Since you're thought to have been a target of these people and the timing suggests your reappearance may have triggered the call, you need to be on the alert."

"Someone who worked for the killer in Nevada?"

"As his secretary, yes. He disappeared right after the parade on President's Day after destroying evidence. We looked for him, of course. There's some speculation he was the driver of the car who struck and killed his supposed employer." Struthers looked through his papers again and showed Alex a photograph of a bald sixty-something-year-old man with a haughty look in his slate eyes. "While he was in Shatterhorn, he used the name William Tucker but we now know that was a stolen identity. We're also pretty sure he shaved his head and isn't really bald. We're not sure what his part was or if it was pivotal. The fact he's been in contact with a man assumed to be involved in a similar militia group in the northwest is what's troubling."

This time when Jessica looked at Alex it was with horror in her eyes instead of impatience. "How do you guys know it was the same man?" she asked.

"He referred to himself as 'aka William Tucker.'"

"And in this conversation, they mentioned a nameless third person, someone here in Blunt Falls?" Alex asked.

"Yes."

Jessica hugged herself. “Is this about money or something? What does someone here have to gain?”

“It’s not about money,” Struthers said. “These people work for ideals, not cash. And it seems to be bipartisan, as well. This is across-the-board terrorism.”

“We have an alarm system in the house and we’ll be sure to use it,” Alex said.

“Just be cautious. Our experience with this strain of domestic militia is that they use any means to make their point, no matter who they kill or maim.”

“And what about the threat of a Memorial Day massacre of sorts? Is that still on people’s minds?”

“Of course. This is the first national holiday since the killer’s botched attempt to gun down people at an Idaho parade on President’s Day. Now with this latest news of a contact here in Blunt Falls, everyone is gearing up to safeguard any festivities.”

“Blunt Falls always has a parade on Memorial Day,” Jessica commented.

He checked his papers again. “I see we’ve discussed this with the mayor and the chief of police, a Mr. Frank Smyth. Measures are being taken both here and in Seattle. Frankly, police all over the country are gearing up with extra precautions.” Struthers shook his head. “The truth is no one is safe anywhere until this current crop of lunatics is put out of business."

"And are you any closer to accomplishing that goal?" Jessica asked.

"We look into every allegation and possibility. It's like any war on terror—many of the victories go unheralded, but that doesn't mean they aren't significant. But malls and parades and both foot and auto races—anything where people gather in large numbers—are being watched."

Alex nodded as he attempted to return the photo, but Struthers shook his head. "You keep it. If you see this guy, call us."

"Do you want us to show it around?"

"Couldn't hurt," the agent said. "But tell people not to approach him, just to get in contact with the FBI. We don't know yet if this man is dangerous or a loose cannon or what exactly he is."

Alex put the photo in his desk, then walked to Jessica's side and laid a hand on her shoulder as he stared into her eyes. It suddenly seemed totally irrelevant that she had somehow doubted his plane crash, that she'd written that damn comment on Facebook for the world to see. He couldn't bear to see pain or fear on her face and he sure as hell wasn't going to go out of his way to create more of it. "I would never let anyone hurt you or our baby," he said softly.

She looked up at him. "Oh, Alex, it's not me or the baby I'm worried about. It's you."

AFTER THE AGENT LEFT, Jessica insisted she needed to work on the test papers she'd brought home from school and promised to lock all the doors and turn on the alarm system. On a whim, he called his doctor who was also a friend. "I've been reading about your triumphant return," Josh Woodward said. "Sounds as if I should check you out."

"That's why I'm calling," Alex said. "I want to go back to work as soon as possible and that means I need a once-over from you. I know it's Saturday, but is there any chance we could do it today?"

"Well, the clinic is open for free vaccinations this afternoon which means there will be a limited staff present. Sure, I'll meet you down there in an hour. You'll have to come back in the next week or so for blood work and any tests I might want to run."

"That's fine, Josh. I'll see you in an hour."

The afternoon was filled with steps toward reaching his goal of getting back to work. After meeting with the doctor, Alex braved the mall to replace the cell phone he'd lost during his months in the mountains, and to get a haircut. Then he took the doctor's clearance to the precinct where he found the place running on a skeleton crew. Maybe crime was lurking on the threshold of Blunt

Falls like the FBI warned, or maybe it wasn't. The sparsely occupied office certainly seemed to suggest the latter.

He left his medical clearance on Chief Smyth's desk, before calling Jessica to tell her he was on his way home. He was not going to fall into the old pattern of coming and going as he pleased, leaving her to guess when he'd show up. She asked him to stop by the store and that's how he found himself peering into the freezer case of their local megamart. He needed something called Moonie Mocha Fudge Ripple. He was determined to find the exact ice cream Jessica had asked for as it was his first experience with the cravings of pregnancy and he didn't want to blow it.

Of course it was chocolate, what else would it be? He finally found the right one and bought two. Then he added a couple of jars of pickles and some anchovies to the order, hoping she'd find that funny, hoping it would ease some of the tension between them.

He paused before going inside the house, determined that tonight he would be honest and clear with her. She deserved no less and, face it, unless he learned how to trust her, sooner or later she was going to walk away and not look back, and that thought was so terrible it made him ache.

He suspected anyone who had lived through years of trying to have a baby didn't take a moment of pregnancy for granted, never assumed everything would turn out right. The worry was always there. He could see it in Jessica's eyes and he could feel it in his own heart.

A minute later, he unlocked his front door and stopped short. A crowd had gathered in the room and they were all staring at him, all grinning. He was so flabbergasted to find his living room full of people that he couldn't make sense of it. And then they yelled "Surprise!" at the same moment and the faces took identities—neighbors, fellow officers and friends from years before. Jessica approached and he handed her the grocery bag as the room instantly filled with music and noise.

"You didn't really need this stuff, did you?" he asked.

"Not really. People were still arriving when you called so I gave you an errand. Are you surprised?"

"I'm stunned," he said truthfully.

"I hope it's okay," she added, her brow furrowed a little. "Your family wanted to come but it was too far away for such short notice. They wanted me to tell you they're coming to Blunt Falls right after Memorial Day."

"I know. My mother called me twice."

"You can't blame her for being relieved you're alive and well."

"I realize that. And everything here is perfect,"

he assured her, anxious to chase away her worry. So what if he would have preferred a quiet evening alone with her? He leaned down and kissed her soft cheek and people applauded, of all things.

"I like your haircut," she added, then kissed his cheek and went to put away the ice cream.

He was flattered by the attention and uneasy with it, too. He'd never craved the limelight nor did he relish repeating his survival story, but he did it anyway, kind of moving into a rote pattern as people asked the same questions over and over. Was he injured in the crash? Had he known search planes were looking for him? What did he eat? How did he survive the snow and freezing conditions? How did he finally manage to escape and make his way to civilization?

And the hardest one of all: What was it like to be home?

The part with Jessica? As well as could be expected leaning cautiously toward great. The part where he'd learned someone may have wanted him dead and might even try again? Not so good.

As the evening wore on and people with younger kids returned to their own homes, Alex found himself in a group of his fellow officers, many of them in uniform as they had shifts to start soon or had just come off of one. Dylan suggested he and the other officers in attendance go outside and Alex wondered if his partner had noticed his discomfort indoors. He hoped not. He didn't want Jessica to see it.

"Before we go outside, I want you guys to look at a photo," he said and they all followed him into his den where he produced the photograph of the man Struthers said might be involved in whatever mayhem was brewing. "I imagine the FBI will share all this with the department if they haven't already, but just in case, I wanted to give you guys a head's up."

"Smug-looking cuss," Dylan said. "Who is he?"

"I'll explain in a minute. Let's go outside, okay?" Alex said, and tucked the photo back into his desk drawer.

The weather had deteriorated in the past few hours and the stars Alex so longed to see had been swallowed up by swirling ground fog that brought a sense of chilled dampness. Still, they settled gamely on the wicker furniture Jessica had somehow taken out of storage while he was gone that day. Obviously, she had not stayed inside with the alarm set or spent her time poring over her students' math papers.

Kit Anderson was the officer who was going to lose his chance at promotion now that Alex was back and he was the first one to speak. "So, I heard you went into work today to make sure you still had a job," he said.

Alex stared at the dark form of his fellow officer. The man's deep voice was tinged with anger. . . . Maybe Dylan had underestimated how much a promotion meant to Kit.

"What did you expect him to do?" Carla Herrera said.

"I don't know," Kit grumbled.

"Just be patient," she added. "Your turn will come."

Alex studied his folded hands and took a deep breath. A cool breeze blew under the eaves, whisking away the smoke from Chief Smyth's cigarette. The chief had arrived an hour ago with his very own newspaper reporter in tow. He'd posed for a couple of pictures with his arm around Alex's shoulders, made a small speech about miracles and was now lingering long after the reporter had gone off to meet his deadline. The man was obviously lobbying for the job of chief to become his on a permanent basis. The glow from the end of a burning cigarette marked his location off to the side. The other officer present was a guy Alex just met. Hank Jones was a new hire and seemed to be on the quiet side.

Alex felt some of the tension in his neck and shoulders ease as he settled against the wicker. They talked shop for a while and then Alex told them about the visit from the FBI. It was too dark to see expressions, but he could feel a watchful current ebb and flow as he spoke. "The bottom line is that we're supposed to be cautious while they try to track this person. There's concern he or she is close by. I'm not worried about myself so much, but I would greatly appreciate everyone keeping their eyes open. I don't want Jessica scared or hurt and I can't watch her 24/7."

"Of course we'll help," Carla Herrera said amid a chorus of assenting voices.

"Thanks."

"So they really think your plane was rigged to crash?" Carla asked.

"It looks like it."

"What do you think?"

"I don't know. I mean, I've thought about what happened and I can't make it anybody's fault. I just wasn't myself that day. In fact, I'd thought for a while that I might have been getting whatever stomach bug Jessica said she had." He laughed softly to himself. "Unless I'm the only pregnant man in the world, that obviously wasn't the case."

"So do you remember every moment like it happened in slow motion?" Smyth asked.

"Not really," Alex admitted. "I hadn't slept well the night before." He'd been up arguing with Jess, but he didn't add that part. "And then I got a late start. Well, you remember, Kit, you called me at the last minute for something. I honestly can't remember what."

"Just an address," Kit Anderson said. "I was

taking over the Hannigan case while you were gone and I didn't know where the guy's girlfriend was staying."

"That's right, now I remember," Alex said. "Anyway, maybe Nate is right. Maybe I was so disorganized I missed something."

Again, that undercurrent of alarm stirred the air around them. Well, it was an alarming situation.

"But why did anyone want the three of you dead in the first place?" Kit asked.

Dylan spoke up. "Because Mike Donovan had called them to go back to Shatterhorn and help him figure out if there was a conspiracy, which we all now know there was." His voice sounded impatient as though this was old news which it was, at least for almost everyone but Alex. "Mike was killed for his trouble, Nate Matthews was wounded and the speculation is that Alex's plane was tampered with. All by a bunch of patriotic zealots."

"Yeah, I remember now," Kit grumbled, and they all fell into a pronounced and prolonged silence.

Finally, Alex heard the creak of the gate across the wooded yard and wondered who was arriving just as things were breaking up. Sitting forward, he strained to see through the fog. A person approached, footsteps crunching on the gravel. Whether it was the effect of the fog or a matter of stature, the figure appeared short and a trifle squat, wearing bulky clothes, walking with hesitant steps. There was something about that walk and the emerging shape that struck Alex as both familiar and a little spooky.

"Can I help you?" Alex called as the person stopped shy of the steps. Who was it?

"Mr. Foster, is that you?"

Recognition came in a rush. Billy Summers, Jessica's ex-student. And the way he'd walked through the fog just now had triggered another recollection for Alex, but this one drifted outside his grasp. No matter, it would come eventually.

"Yes, it's me," Alex said. "You're a little late for the party."

"Then it's true, you really are alive," Billy said, his whisper tinged with awe.

"Yeah, it's true. How can I help you?"

"I have to tell you something," he said in a rush.

"Sure. Come on up onto the porch." Alex turned in the direction of the burning cigarette and added, "Chief, switch on that other light there by the door so Billy can see his way up here. Come on, Billy, have a seat and speak your mind."

The light went on and everyone blinked against the sudden illumination, even though the fog diffused the brightness. Alex looked down the three shallow steps. Billy was staring up in alarm, his gaze traveling from one officer to the next, eyes wide, mouth agape. It came to Alex suddenly that the kid hadn't realized there were other people on the porch.

Billy had to be about twenty now, a guy with a round face and perpetually pink cheeks. His shaggy brown hair flopped over his forehead and down his neck and was mostly covered by an old cap whose logo had all but disappeared under layers of oil and grease. He was dressed in a black T-shirt and jeans with a dark green windbreaker over all.

"Go ahead and get comfortable, Billy," Alex said. "I want to thank you for all the work you did on this yard while I was gone. It meant a lot to my wife and to me, too. And it will mean a lot to the families of the veterans come Memorial Day. Now, what can I do for you?"

"Mama told me you got back," he said with a sideways glance at Alex and away. He wasn't the brightest guy in town, but he was always friendly and pretty reliable. There was no doubt he had his share of burdens to deal with. Besides his own learning impairments, his mother was a difficult woman who had once been a great beauty. She'd married an out-of-work mill worker right out of high school but the guy died a few weeks after Billy was born. After his death, rumors circulated she slept around, but slowly those gossipy whispers were replaced by ones concerning her descent into some kind of undefined mental issues that now kept her more or less trapped in the double-wide she shared with her only son. Billy took care of her as well as doing odd jobs at the airport. Money had to be tight.

"She must have read it in the newspaper," Alex said.

"She likes to collect newspapers," Billy said, his gaze lifting to meet the intense interest of the other officers, then sliding away. When Smyth cleared his throat, Billy jumped a few inches.

Smyth was fiftysomething, with a shaved head and a hooked, prominent nose with a tight, strong body thanks to weekend trail biking. His unblinking gaze sometimes reminded Alex of a hawk. Given the cornered look on Billy's face, he agreed with that assessment.

Billy swallowed and tried talking a couple of times, but the sentences ended in stuttering and were difficult to understand. Alex tried to get him to sit down, but he wouldn't or couldn't, nor did he recover his ability to speak coherently. He paced a little, stared at Dylan, paced some more, stared at Herrera, paced some more, darted a quick glance at Chief Smyth.

During this uncomfortable interlude, Alex had a sudden memory of the day his plane lifted off the Blunt Falls runway, something he had completely put out of his mind until that moment of watching Billy aimlessly move around the porch while darting looks this way and that. Add the vision he'd created earlier when he walked through the fog and it suddenly gelled. "You were at the airfield," he said to Billy.

Billy stopped pacing so abruptly he almost tripped on his own feet. "What?" he said.

"Yeah, you were there," Alex said. "In fact, when I came out of the office after taking Kit's call, you were on the field. You'd been deicing someone's windshield, remember? You were carrying the equipment and you were walking toward me during a light snow flurry. In fact, you're the last person I saw that day."

The kid's Adam's apple slid up and down his throat as he swallowed.

"You don't remember seeing Alex?" Dylan asked, hands planted on his knees.

"I forget," the boy said, swallowing yet again. Little beads of perspiration sprang out across his forehead and the redness in his cheeks paled.

"Sounds to me like you're hiding something," the chief said.

"No, no, nothing," Billy sputtered.

"Then why did you come here tonight?"

"I've been helping…helping…you know…Mrs. Foster…with yard work."

"At eleven o'clock at night?"

"No. No. Mama told me Mr. Foster came home. I wanted to see if he was okay, that's all."

"You said you wanted to tell him something," Herrera said.

"I don't remember," Billy said quickly, his voice high and anxious.

The porch door opened and Jessica appeared carrying a tray laden with tall cups of what smelled like coffee, probably in deference to those who still had hours of work ahead of them. Her warm smile faded a bit as her gaze settled on the obvious distress of Billy's expression. Cups slid as the tray dipped. Alex grabbed it from her just in time.

"What's going on?" she asked as he settled the tray on a table.

"Billy came to talk to me," he said.

She looked at the formidable group facing the young man and stepped forward. "Did you ride your bike into town this late at night and in the fog?" she asked Billy, casting him a kindly look.

"Yes, ma'am," he squeaked.

"Would you like something hot to drink?"

"No," he said. "I've got to go."

"Okay," she said softly. "But be careful on that road, okay?"

He nodded, his gaze downcast.

"Come back tomorrow when you remember what you wanted," Alex added.

"Yeah, okay," he said, but he wasted no time hustling down the stairs to beat a hasty retreat toward the gate. The fog swallowed him up after just a few steps.

Jessica looked after him with confusion on her face. "That was odd. He's not usually forgetful."

"The boy couldn't get his thoughts straight if he wanted to," the chief said. "But looking at what I can see of your garden amazes me. Who would have thought the kid had this kind of beauty in him?" He dropped his cigarette butt and ground it out beneath his heel. "The wife just got back from spending a week with our daughter at her college. I guess I'd better get home. And by the way, Alex, I saw your medical clearance on my desk when I stopped by the precinct on my way over here. We'll see you bright and early Monday morning, okay?"

Alex grinned. "You bet."

"I'll walk you out," Jessica said, and led the chief back into the house. He'd arrived late and he'd used the front entrance. No backyard gates for him.

Dylan got to his feet and heaved a deep breath. "I think the party's over."

"THANK YOU FOR TONIGHT," Alex said as he got ready for bed.

Sitting at her dresser and brushing her hair, Jessica glanced in the mirror where she saw Alex's reflection. "Did you really like it?"

"What was not to like?" he said which she took as a nonanswer.

"Oh, I don't know. After being alone for so long, all these people might have been difficult for you to handle all at once. Maybe I shouldn't have tried to surprise you."

"You did what you thought best," he said. "It was fine."

It was on the tip of her tongue to tell him to stop making nice all the time. She knew he was worried the peace they seemed to have found was too fragile to withstand brutal honesty, but he'd have to get over it if they stood a chance at a real marriage. "How about Chief Smyth bringing a reporter?" she asked, shaking her head. "What is that guy's problem?"

"My guess is that he was trying to score points with the mayor by getting his picture front and center in Sunday's newspaper. The reporter had the look of a guy making a few extra bucks."

She turned to face him, watching as he unbuttoned his shirt. "That was odd about Billy, wasn't it?"

"Yeah. But he's always been a little awkward with people."

"I think seeing all you cops must have unnerved him."

"That's what I thought. All of us have been out

to his mother's place a few times over the years. She's had her share of trouble."

He pulled his shirt off, stood up and unbuttoned his jeans. He was leaner than she'd ever seen him, but stronger, too, the muscles in his chest and shoulders honed by the work he'd been doing to stay alive. She couldn't really imagine what he'd gone through, how he'd survived the first few days of storms and snow with a badly injured leg and cuts on his face. She'd asked him to tell her in greater detail, but he'd glossed over all the facts, dismissing the experience as yesterday's news.

He paused as he sat back down on the edge of the mattress, just in his boxers now. There were scars running up and down his left leg that made her wince when she thought of the agony he must have endured all by himself. And yet he looked younger than he had in years, and incredibly handsome. Every molecule in her body reminded her that making love to him was about the best thing in the whole entire world.

"He was fine until the lights came on," Alex mused. "When he saw everyone he just clammed up. Do you have any idea what he wanted?"

"No," she said. "He's been coming around like I told you, but he doesn't talk a whole lot."

"That's the feeling I got," Alex said. "Oh, and I

recalled seeing him at the airport the morning I flew out of here, though he claimed he didn't remember."

"He'll come back tomorrow, then we'll know," she said, getting up from the small chair and walking to the bed where she sat beside him. "Thanks for the anchovies and pickles," she whispered.

He looked into her eyes. "I know how you love anchovies," he said.

She smiled as she bumped his shoulder with hers.

"I'm sorry about not telling you that Nate and I made those plans," he added.

"We got used to keeping things to ourselves," she said. "We have to unlearn all those bad habits."

"Are you going to get mad at me every time I try to protect you?"

"Probably," she said. "I know how you feel," she admitted. "I feel the same way. We've had our problems, Alex, but I've never stopped loving you."

He smiled. "I'm glad to hear that." He raised his hand and ran his fingers through her hair, his gaze devouring her. She closed the distance between them and touched his lips with hers. His were tender, his mouth hot and sexy.

"I've missed you so much," he murmured.

"I've missed you, too," she whispered, and realized as the words left her lips that they were true. She missed the man she'd once known, the man who had loved her, the man she'd trusted with her life and happiness. And now it seemed he was willing to try to find that man again. She knew she'd grown distant, too. They both needed to work.

"I want to make love to you," he said against her ear.

His warm breath traveled through her body like a renegade spark, awakening torrid memories of endless nights of bliss as it burned under her skin. The temptation to give in to her desire for him sent her heart racing and it took a few seconds to trust herself to speak. "I'm not ready," she whispered at last. "I need to think with my head, not my heart and certainly not my body. You know what you do to me."

He smiled slowly. "It's mutual."

"We'll get there," she said softly, and then took a chance that the changes she sensed in him were real. "Being pregnant has reminded me how much I want children," she said, meeting his gaze. "Alex, if I lose this baby, then I want to adopt. You wouldn't even talk about it before, but that's the decision I've reached and I hope you'll at least discuss it with me."

"If you lose this baby," he said, his voice thick, "then I'm open to adoption."

"Just like that?"

"Let's just say that spending one hundred and

three nights alone with nothing to do but try to stay warm gives you plenty of time to think. And what I realized was that life is a gift, that living with someone you cherish is a gift. I don't get to call every shot, I have to roll with the punches, we all do. If adoption is the best way to grow our family, then I'm on board. Let's get the pitter-patter of little feet running around here."

She blinked away warm tears. "Thank you," she whispered.

He shifted his weight and settled back on his side of the bed. "Come here," he said, and she scooted up beside him. He pulled her against his chest and flicked off the light.

His skin was warm and musky smelling. He kept running his hand up and down her bare arm, kissing her hair and she closed her eyes, trying to relax. Eventually, she could tell by his breathing that he'd fallen asleep and she was glad.

She'd known the minute he walked in the door tonight that a party was the absolute last thing in the world he wanted. Whereas she'd found the noise and laughter of friends and family comforting after the dire news Agent Struthers delivered, she suspected Alex had found it intrusive.

Thank goodness they'd have tomorrow before the rat race of his job and the last few weeks of teaching hit full force. It seemed forever since she'd had a nice, normal, boring day.

Several hours later, the ringing phone woke her with a start. Alex fumbled with the light and grabbed the receiver as Jessica sat up in bed. No good news ever seemed to come when it was still dark outside. The clock read 5:00 a.m.

Alex spoke in a surprisingly crisp voice, which suggested he was already awake. He hung up abruptly and looked at her. "That was weird," he said.

"Who was it?"

"Frank Smyth. He asked me to go out to Billy's place. Since I'm not technically back at work, he's hoping I can keep the visit under the radar. Don't ask me why."

"Is something wrong?"

"I'm not sure. I guess the chief got a call from Billy's mom but he wasn't explicit about what she said. You know how the chief worries about his public image.... I guess that's why he wants to handle it this way." He leaned over and kissed her lips. "I'll be back before you know it."

"I'm going with you," she said.

"Absolutely not," he said, pulling on his jeans.

She was already out of bed and looking through her drawer for jeans of her own.

"Jess, I'm serious," he insisted. "I don't want you to come."

"You don't want me in any danger," she said,

stepping into leggings. Her jeans had been getting a little tight in the waist lately.

"Of course I don't want you in danger," he said.

"From Billy's mother? Really? Anyway, you'll protect me," she said on her way to brush her teeth.

"This is police business," he announced as though that sealed his argument.

"No, it's not," she called from the bathroom, then turned to look back into the bedroom. "Smyth asked you to take care of it because you're not on the roster yet." She watched Alex open the gun safe as she started brushing. He took out his service pistol and put it in a shoulder holster, which he strapped over his T-shirt. They passed in the bathroom door as he went in and she came out.

She shrugged on a light sweater and slipped her feet into moccasins. "Why would she call the chief directly?" Jessica asked as she gathered her hair into a quick ponytail.

"I have no idea," Alex said as he set aside a hand towel. "He just said he couldn't take the call. I don't know why, but I got the feeling he wasn't even at his house."

"His wife just came home, where else would he be? Anyway, the reason I'm going with you is that Billy trusts me. He'll be more likely to talk if I'm there."

"I don't even know if Billy is there."

"Where else would he be?" she repeated as she

walked out of the bedroom. After a few steps, she called over her shoulder, "Are you coming?"

She heard him swear under his breath as he caught up with her. It sounded like he said, "Damn stubborn woman." She laughed out loud. At least they'd finally had a genuine honest moment.

Chapter Four

Back when Alex had been on patrol, he'd been called out a number of times to the Summers house for various disturbances. Nothing serious, just one of those situations where occasional loud arguments, late-night noises and unbelievable clutter brought complaints from neighbors.

The last time he'd seen Lynda Summers had been a good three or four years before. That time, neighbors had called because of the five old broken-down cars in her front yard and a putrid rotting smell emanating from the shed out back. It turned out the shed housed dozens of sacks of garbage and at least one dead opossum.

The road that led out to her place was called Blue Point but he often thought it should have a more ominous name as it was narrow and twisty, a challenge to manipulate on a foggy morning before the sun had a chance to burn it away. By the time he and Jessica pulled into the front drive of their destination, they were both tense from the trip.

The lights in the house shone through the fog as the door opened and Lynda Summers stepped outside. “Where’s Frank?” she demanded.

“He couldn’t make it,” Alex told her.

Lynda was edging toward fifty. Time and hard living had eroded her prom-queen looks, though she still exuded an earthy quality. Her hair was now all but colorless, wispy and fine, overprocessed. At five-thirty in the morning, she wore an ivory housedress and fuzzy slippers that might have once been white. The overall result was unbelievable paleness.

However, much more distracting than her appearance was the way she had of regarding people with her head tilted and one eye kind of half-shut, as though she was trying to discern everything they were hiding. It was unsettling, to say the least. Even the most virtuous person in the world doesn’t appreciate being looked at as if he’s a sleazeball.

“I know who you are,” she said at last. “You’re that cop who disappeared. You used to come out here and give me trouble, didn’t you? You cops, I swear, you’re all alike. Your picture was in the paper yesterday. You look pretty good for a dead man.”

“That’s because I’m not dead,” he said, attempting humor.

“Everyone thought you were.” She cast a long look at Jessica before looking back at him. “Why do I get the feeling you were really hiding? Not that I'd blame you. I think about doing that sometimes."

"What?" he said incredulously. "I wasn't hiding. The paper explained about the crash."

"You can't believe the things you read," she said. "But I didn't call you. I called Frank. A long time ago, too."

"And Frank called me," Alex said.

"That jerk." She turned suddenly and, moving way faster than it appeared she could, retreated into her house. Since she didn't close the door, Alex and Jessica hesitantly followed.

"What's the problem?" Alex asked, stopping right inside the door because that was about as far as he could get. Piles and heaps of clothes, stuffed animals, books, magazines, newspapers, dishes and every other possible thing took up all the floor space, except for a couple of narrow paths carved out of the junk that ran down the middle of the room and a path to a love seat and chair situated in front of a television. Some of the walls were covered with sagging shelves crammed with dolls. All those glassy eyes staring endlessly were creepy. Even doorways sported mounds of objects that seemed to burst through the openings like lava from an inferno's fissures. Alex's gut clenched. Being inside was hard for him anyway, and being inside this closed junk pile felt suffocating.

Lynda gave him her one eyed stare as she watched his gaze travel her home. She didn't respond to the question and he wondered if she'd heard him.

Right behind him, Jessica cleared her throat. "Mrs. Summers, is Billy here?"

Lynda's attention turned to Jessica. "I don't think so," she said, stopping to pick up a paper sack full of what looked like dolls still in their boxes and mindlessly setting it back down. "You're that teacher, aren't you. Well, last I saw of him he was headed out to your house."

"He got there about eleven last night," Alex said, "but he claimed he forgot why he came. Do you know why he wanted to see us?"

She shrugged. "He spent the day moping around, muttering to himself like he does. You can't get a decent conversation out of him when he's like that."

"He left our house hours ago," Jessica added. "Are you saying he never arrived home?"

"Maybe he's in his bedroom." Lynda gestured at the doorway Alex had seen earlier, the one piled with junk. Moving carefully through the mess, he approached the door along a little side track, picking his way over discarded clothes. He could see where someone consistently climbed over the pile in the doorway. He found a switch and flicked it on, illuminating a sea of junk. How could anyone sleep in this?

A quick look around revealed a mattress in one far corner with a little lamp on the floor beside it. A couple of blankets and a comic book lay abandoned on the "bed."

"Is he in there?" Lynda called.

Alex retraced his steps. "No."

"Aren't you worried about him?" Jessica asked. "It's very foggy outside and he was on a bike."

"You don't have any kids do you?" Lynda snapped.

"Not yet," Jessica said, as her hand seemed to automatically cradle her abdomen.

"Do yourself a favor and skip it. You got yourself a good-looking guy here. Kind of scrawny for my taste, but a hunk anyway. Why mess up a good thing with a bunch of little brats running around? And try getting rid of them when they finally grow up. Look at Billy. He's a full-grown man no matter what people think and I'm still supposed to provide a roof over his head."

Alex saw anger flash in Jessica's eyes, but she held her tongue.

"Anyway, maybe he got tired and stopped at a friend's house."

"What friend?" Alex asked. "Can you give us a name?"

"That mechanic at the airfield. Tony something."

"Tony Machi?"

"I guess. Billy thinks he can learn by osmosis. That'll be the day. Or maybe those look-alike kids."

"What are their names?" Alex asked.

"I don't know. Who cares?"

"Did you call around or go look for him?" Jessica asked.

"How would I do that?" Lynda said. "I don't have a single car that runs. You'd think that worthless son of mine could get one of them to start, but no, he just tinkers and tinkers and nothing ever gets fixed. He better get home soon. There's nothing in this dump to eat."

"Maybe you aren't worried, but I am," Jessica said calmly. "Do either of you know where this Tony lives?"

"I can find out," Alex said.

Lynda shrugged again. "I don't go into town anymore." When she abruptly threw up her hands, one grazed a box to her side. The others jiggled and swayed in a rippling effect that seemed to spread across the top layer from one side of the room to the other like a small tsunami. "Billy will be fine. Stop your bellyaching," she said as she ignored the threatening box over her head.

And that wavering tower was just one of dozens, crowding around the room like soldiers on the warpath, determined to take over the house.

It was a miracle she could survive in this environment. Maybe he needed to talk to social services Monday morning because if ever a house was a fire and health risk, this place was it. For now, he hitched his hands on his waist. “If you aren’t worried about Billy, why did you call Chief Smyth?”

Her answer came in a begrudging voice. “Because I heard a noise out back. It woke me up.”

“What kind of noise?” What he really wanted to know was why she felt free to call Chief Smyth in the middle of the night about something that should have gone through the dispatch desk.

“Someone was out there, probably trying to steal something. I turned on a light and the noise stopped. As long as you’re here, you might as well go take a look. But don’t touch anything.”

“Okay,” he said, determined not to roll his eyes, which was what he wanted to do. The house smelled—how did Jessica keep from heaving? She must not have morning sickness. Still, he touched her arm. “Maybe you should come outside while I look around,” he said figuring she was safer out there with a potential burglar than in here.

“I’ll be fine,” she said, sidling away from the teetering stack of boxes.

“You can’t get outside through the kitchen door,” Lynda said. “It’s blocked. You’ll have to go out the front way and walk around.”

With a last glance at Jessica, he stepped outside

where a deep breath of fresh, damp air reinvigorated him. He dug a small but intense flashlight out of his pocket to help thread his way through the yard, which was almost as cluttered as the inside of the house. Evidence of Billy's automotive endeavors littered the path as three cars that looked as if they hadn't moved in a decade stood parked with their hoods open and various engine parts scattered about. There was no sign that Billy had practiced his green thumb on his mother's land.

The sun was just coming up behind the hills, a yellow glow doing its best to break from under the haze like smothered candlelight. For a minute Alex stopped walking and listened. Birds had begun chirping, tree branches hung low and damp from the mist. There didn't seem to be any unexplained noises. He shined his light on the shed and found a lock securing the door through the hasp to which it was affixed. There were scratch marks and gouges on the wooden door as though someone had tried to pry the lock off. There was no way of telling how old they were.

A lean-to had been erected next to the shed and he shone his light there next. It was stuffed to the top with garbage bags and cardboard boxes, used motor parts and heaven knew what else. The light dispersed several rats who scurried off under the debris.

He backed away and shone the light around the yard one more time. As water dripped down his neck, he found himself shaking his head. What in the world would anyone steal in a place like this? Lynda Summers was absolutely delusional.

He walked back to find Jessica standing on the porch, Lynda still in the house by the door.

"Well?" she demanded.

"It's possible someone tried to enter your shed. It doesn't appear they were successful."

"That was probably Billy's doing," Lynda said. "He keeps his engine parts out there and he's always losing the blasted key. You look like a drowned rat. Go home and tell Frank thanks a lot when you see him."

"Let us know if you have further problems," Alex said as he reached up to take Jessica's hand and help her down the rickety stairs.

"I TRIED TO talk to her about her son and his living conditions while you were outside," Jessica said as they pulled up in front of a diner they'd last frequented years before. It looked to her that it had changed hands. Bright lights and plaid curtains on the windows gave it a homey, welcoming appearance.

"Have any luck?" Alex asked.

"None. I met her years ago when Billy was in my class. She was odd then, she's odder now."

"What an understatement," he said, holding the door open for her. They were greeted by the delicious smells of coffee and bacon. She thought it must be amazing to Alex to be in a restaurant after months of cooking his own food over a campfire.

Alex called around while they waited for their order to be delivered. He jotted down the airport mechanic's phone number on his paper napkin, then called the man. When he hung up, he shook his head.

"Billy has never been to Tony's house," he said. "In fact, Tony sounded surprised I'd even suggest such a thing."

"Maybe Billy has a life his mother knows nothing about," Jessica said. "One that includes friends. After what we saw this morning, I have to say I sincerely hope that's true."

"Yeah."

Jessica took a deep breath. She was going to be a mother soon. She couldn't imagine ever talking about her child as Lynda Summers had talked of Billy.

"What are you going to tell Frank Smyth?"

"Exactly what happened. I'm hoping he volunteers the reason he was in the middle of such a routine call and why he sent a detective out for something that should have been handled by a patrolman. I can't quite make sense of it."

Their food was delivered right as Alex unfolded

the newspaper someone had left on the bench seat. As Jessica buttered her waffle, he groaned. "Look at this," he said, holding the paper so she could see the photo below the fold. There was Chief Smyth with his arm around Alex's shoulder and a big grin on his face. "Chief Frank Smyth welcomes home Detective Alex Foster," the blurb beneath it announced.

"Good heavens," Jessica said.

"There's a whole recap of the same story they ran Saturday," Alex said. "People are going to be sick of me if this keeps up."

She put down her fork as he sliced a bite of melon. "Alex, how did you catch the fish you ate? How did you cook them?"

"I found fishing gear in the emergency kit I salvaged," he said after swallowing. "Of course, it was touch and go for a few days when I was too sick to fish, but eventually I cooked on spits or flat rocks. The stuff I walked out with, I dried and smoked."

"I wish I had been with you," she mused aloud. "Not because it was a picnic, mind you, just because I could have helped."

"I thanked God every single day that you weren't on that plane," he said seriously.

"How did you keep from getting lost?"

"There was a compass in the emergency bag. The trail between the lake and the camp was marked with a forked tree at the lake side, so it wasn't too hard. What with my leg and everything, I didn't exactly wander far afield."

She chewed silently for a moment before adding, "We haven't really talked about what Agent Struthers told us yesterday. About the call from Shatterhorn to someone here in Blunt Falls."

"I don't know what we can do about any of it until they figure out who the call was made to. We just have to be extra careful." He paused before adding, "Would you consider flying to Kansas City to stay with your sister for a few weeks until this is over?"

"No," she said.

"But—"

"But nothing. I just got you back, I'm not leaving." She didn't add that if she left, she might have nothing to come back to. The threat from some nameless, faceless person coupled with the threat of losing her marriage made leaving impossible for her. "We're in this together, as a family," she said.

He nodded and she was shocked he didn't pursue it. Pleased, but shocked. "Okay," she continued. "Let's move from looming disaster to more mundane things. How about helping me change the batteries in all the smoke alarms today? You weren't here on the first day of spring when we usually do it and I didn't want to ask Billy."

"Sure. But now that you've brought up Billy, I

was just thinking that he never came around our house before I crashed the Cessna."

"I know. I hadn't seen him since high school, but like I told you, two or three days after the crash, he showed up and asked if I needed help shoveling snow. Once I gave in and agreed, I tried to pay him, but he wouldn't take any money. How he rode from his place to our house in the snow on that old red bike is a mystery, but he did."

They left the café holding hands. The wind had come up and cut through the fog, made the parking lot a cold, damp, nasty place. Once they got to the car, he turned her to face him. "Do you need to go anywhere else before we head home?"

"Nope." She noticed that he scanned the parking lot every few moments, looking for bad guys, she supposed. She looked around, too. What people were visible through the mist seemed in a hurry to get out of the weather. No one seemed to have a good tan like the man in the photograph.

"Let's just go home and do chores like normal people," he said at last as he turned his gaze to her. His hazel eyes seemed to glow and she realized that each day he was back seemed to erase a week of the time he'd been gone. He was growing familiar again, closer, like before the Labor Day mall shooting and even way before that.

He kissed her forehead and she smiled. "Watch what you say," she warned him, touching his forehead where a pink welt was all that remained of the cut she knew he'd received when the plane landed and he was hit by broken glass. "I happen to have accumulated a long list."

"Great," he said. "Just make sure there's time in there for us to take a nap in the hammock if it ever warms up, okay?"

"And to talk to Billy when he comes by," she added.

"If he comes by."

FOR THE SECOND morning in a row, Alex awoke to the sound of a ringing phone. He answered it quickly, noting as he did that the fog was gone, replaced by heavy, thunderous-looking clouds. May in Blunt Falls was always a mix of weather.

"Yes," he said.

"The chief just called," Dylan said. "We have a dead body out on Evergreen. I'll be by to pick you up in fifteen minutes."

"I can come get you," Alex said. "It would be faster."

"No, I've moved out beyond your house. Just be ready."

Alex got out of bed as quietly as he could, took a quick shower and pulled on his clothes. It would have been nice to start back to work with something a little less gruesome, but you took what you got.

He leaned over the bed and kissed Jessica awake, knowing the alarm clock would ring within minutes anyway. He'd talked to her last night about making sure the house alarm was set and driving a different route to the school, encouraging her to park near others and not wander around by herself. She'd tolerated his instructions better than he'd thought she would and then reminded him that no one had tried to kill her, so maybe he should take his own advice.

"I have to leave," he told her. "We have a dead body."

"Do you know who it is? Is it Billy?"

"I seriously doubt it. Evergreen is a long way from Blue Point. I'll call you later and let you know my plans."

"Okay."

"And don't forget—"

"To set the alarm when I leave. Yes, dear."

He smiled at her and kissed her forehead.

Dylan pulled up right as Alex walked down the driveway. He got into Dylan's dark gray car and they took off as Alex opened a Vita-Drink and took a swig.

"You still drinking that stuff?"

"It's good for you," Alex said. "I'd think you'd appreciate that. Where'd you move to?"

"Eagle Nest."

Alex whistled. "That's the high-rent district."

"I got a deal. They like having a cop around and I like the on-site gym."

Alex looked at the scratched dashboard and added, "I thought someone said you got a new ride."

"I did," he said.

"This doesn't look real new."

Dylan nodded. "It's not. I drove my car to Billings yesterday for a date."

"That's a long ways to go for a date," Alex said.

"You haven't seen the girl. Man, she's barely out of high school."

"Did you check her age?" Alex said.

"Of course I did. She's legal. Unfortunately, she's also a terrible driver. Got rear-ended, so I had to borrow her car while mine gets fixed. Eight hundred and six miles on the odometer and she puts it in the shop."

"Yeah," Alex said, always amazed at Dylan's desire to bed any female he met. For Alex there was one girl, one woman, and that was Jess. "Time to get to work," he said. "What do we know about our victim?"

Dylan cast him a swift look. "A guy with a metal detector was working the lot at the old drive-in theater when he came across a dead man."

"It's kind of early in the morning for a metal detector isn't it? Was it even light when he was out there?"

"Just barely. It takes all kinds, though. I've run kids out of there plenty of times."

"Maybe they hit someone they didn't know was there," Alex said.

"Maybe. But these kids also do drugs so maybe one of them OD'd and the rest ran off. I'm thinking about the Cummings twins."

The Cummings twins. Was that what Lynda Summers had meant when she said "look-alike" kids? They drove in silence for a moment and then Dylan started talking again. "What did you and Jess do over the weekend?" he asked as he turned onto Evergreen.

"Things around the house."

"I can't believe you're back from near death for two days and Jessica has you doing chores."

"I didn't mind. I just like being with her." He paused a second, thinking back to the day before. "Chief Smyth had me handle an off-the-record complaint from Lynda Summers. She said she heard a noise in her yard."

"Did you find anything?"

"No. Someone might have been trying to break into the shed—I doubt it, though."

"He's had me run out there a handful of times in the past few weeks, too," Dylan said. "What a pigsty."

Alex cast him a long look. "Same kind of thing?"

"Yeah. Almost always it's nothing I can do

much about. Last time it was because she was mad at a neighbor who told her they were going to turn her in if she didn't fix up her yard. She wanted me to go read them the riot act. I walked over and calmed down the neighbor. Face it, the Summers house belongs on one of those reality TV shows."

"How did the chief ever get on the receiving end of her calls?

"Believe it or not, his mother is responsible. He told me this one night after a couple of beers. His mother was Lynda's godmother. The old lady—on her deathbed, mind you—made Frank promise to take over as Lynda's unofficial guardian angel. By then Lynda was getting a little goofy. He did as good as he could when he was a detective like you and me, but it was impossible to protect her from everything. Now he's acting chief and he seems hell-bent on making sure her antics fly under the radar."

"I'm not sure he's doing Lynda a favor by helping her avoid reality," Alex mused. "It's a wonder something hasn't fallen on her head and crushed her to death."

"Yeah," Dylan said, "but since Smyth is obviously aware of her predicament, I've decided to mind my own business."

They finally glimpsed vehicles and lights up ahead all pulled into the giant parking lot of the old drive-in theater. Dylan drove slowly through the open gates.

Kit Anderson was one of the uniforms who had responded to the panicked metal detector's call. He had on rain gear which he might very well need within the hour. "We've got guys combing the area for any evidence," he said by way of greeting.

"Get them into a grid," Alex said. "Try to cover the whole lot before the weather breaks."

"Where's the guy with the metal detector?" Dylan asked.

"In the back of my car. He was pretty shook up. His name is Henry Fields and he admits he comes here once or twice a year to see if he can find anything interesting. He says he always wiggles through some loose boards in the back so he didn't notice the chain on the front entrance had been cut."

"Why in the world did he come out here so early?" Alex asked.

"I asked him that. He says there's never anyone around out here when it rains, so as soon as he got up and heard the weather report, he took off. His truck is parked out behind the lot where he left it."

"We'll go talk to him," Alex said.

Kit shook his head. "There's no need," he said. "He already told me everything he knows." Kit was a tall, wiry man who had been a track-and-field star back in high school. He gestured with a long arm. "If I were you, I'd go talk to the M.E.," he suggested, his voice on the raw edge of condescending. "He's been here for quite a while."

"But you aren't me," Alex said softly. "Please join the search and set up a grid, okay?"

"Sure," Kit said, and walked off with a scowl.

"You got yourself an enemy," Dylan said as they moved toward the squad car.

"I guess. I don't want him pissed at me all the time, but there's not a lot I can do because I didn't wind up moldering away in the mountains."

"Are you thinking Kit had something to do with that crash?"

"Hell, no. I didn't say that."

"Because I can't imagine he'd go to such lengths."

"Nor can I." Alex stopped abruptly. "You know, though, in this case he may be right. We both don't need to question our metal detector. I'll go get started on the crime scene before the weather deteriorates."

"Sounds good," Dylan said, and ambled toward the squad car.

Alex approached the crowd of people gathered under an open tent. He'd come to this theater a few times when he was a kid but it had closed decades ago. There was no longer a standing screen or a concession/projector building, just gently rolling ground. In the old days, cars would pull their front ends up on the berms, giving them a clear line of sight to the big outdoor screen over the tops of the cars in front of them. Remnants of metal posts that used to hold the speakers stuck up out of the weeds.

Patrolmen had erected a tent over the body in deference to the deteriorating weather. The victim was facedown in one of the lower spots between the humps. Thanks to the team working the scene, he couldn't see the dead man, just a pile of what appeared to be mangled dark clothing amid a sea of flashbulbs.

"Someone ran over him," the M.E. said as he approached Alex. "More than once, I might add." He turned to the ambulance crew and called, "I'm finished for now. You can get the Vic ready for transport."

"Do we have an ID?" Alex asked.

"Not yet. We've taken his prints, but right now all I can tell you is we have a Caucasian male in his early twenties. There's no sign he struggled, which leads me to believe he was unconscious when he was run over."

"Any signs of drugs?"

"No, but I'll run a toxicology."

"How about a time of death?"

He shook his graying head which was covered with a jaunty plaid beret. "At least twenty-four hours. He's been here awhile."

So he'd died sometime early Sunday morning. Alex thought for a moment before speculating. "I wonder if he walked out here, overdosed on something and fell into a deep sleep or hit his head." Like Dylan said, teens sometimes cut through the chain and came in here at night to race over the rolling lot, seeing just how fast they could go and most of the time, they did it late enough there were few people to see their headlights. If there'd been a sleeping or drugged person in a dark spot, it was conceivable someone ran over him accidentally. However, you'd think they would have noticed a bump and quit after the first hit.

"I'll know more after the autopsy," the M.E. said.

Alex nodded as he looked around. The ground was covered with a layer of weeds that would make getting tire impressions tricky even if it hadn't been raining most of the night.

Alex pulled up his collar as more rain started now. He began the trek down to the body but before he got far, Kit Anderson yelled from the back of the lot near where the screen used to be. Alex changed direction and jogged through the rain. He stopped short as he got close enough to see what had been found near a pile of discarded lumber: a mangled red bicycle.

"I don't think it's been here long," Kit said as Officer Herrera planted an evidence flag near the bike and the photographer began snapping pictures. "There's no rust to speak of."

"Get something over it as quick as you can," Alex said, then turned and retraced his steps. They were loading the body into the ambulance as he gently pulled the blanket away from the victim's face.

Somewhere in his gut he'd known.

"Oh, Billy," he whispered. "What in the hell did you get yourself into?"

Chapter Five

"Take me by the school," Alex told Dylan.

"Jessica's school? Why?"

"Because I don't want her to hear about Billy from someone else."

"Then call her," Dylan said with his typical lack of understanding about sensitive issues. No wonder he went through women like water through a sieve.

"Billy Summers was important to Jessica, especially in the last few months. The kid brought some color into her life and I owe it to both of them to make sure she hears what happened to him from me."

"Use the damn phone," Dylan said impatiently.

"Stop at the school. It'll take ten minutes."

Dylan did as asked, immediately taking out his cell and making phone calls as Alex jogged inside. Probably because of the rain, but maybe because of the run across the drive-in lot, his leg hurt today but he ignored the pain.

He found Jessica alone in her classroom as it was late lunch period by now. She was eating a sandwich at her desk while reading a book.

She looked happy to see him, which warmed his heart to no end, and rose to greet him. He hugged her and held her for a moment, breathing in the fragrance of her hair and the feel of her body next to his, simple pleasures he would never take for granted again.

"Why are you here?" she finally asked, and he requested she sit down.

Five minutes later, tears in her eyes, she blew her nose on a tissue Alex fetched for her. "How did Lynda Summers take it?" she asked. Her voice was raw with grief.

"Chief Smyth said she took it hard," he said.

"Do you have any idea who would do this to him?"

"The drive-in gets weekend action from teens driving too fast and doing drugs. Maybe Billy was in the wrong place at the wrong time. Anyway, I just wanted you to know I'll be late tonight and I didn't want you hearing this from someone else."

"Has he been missing since he left our house?" she asked.

"I'm not sure, but it looks like it. Far as I can tell he was wearing the same clothes. I'll talk to his mother later and find out for sure. Are you okay?

I've got a ton to do and Dylan is outside chomping at the bit."

"Go do your job," she said. "And be careful."

"That's what I was going to tell you," he said, and kissed her on the lips. Hers were salty, but sweet, and he hugged her once more.

He didn't tell her about the drug angle Dylan had brought up because he knew she wouldn't believe it, and until verified, it was just a rumor. Dylan had told him he heard that the Cummings twins used Billy like an enforcer of sorts and speculated someone got back at him by giving him some of the drugs and then killing him. Alex just wanted to make sure of the cause of death before they started making up stories.

Within twenty minutes, they were bypassing the air terminal to drive around to the back of the airport. Alex's gaze was drawn to the three rows of privately owned planes and specifically to the spot on the tarmac he'd rented for his Cessna. There was another plane there now.

They parked by the maintenance building and went inside where they found Tony Machi working on the engine of a small aqua-colored single-engine plane Alex knew was owned by a local lawyer. Tony looked up from his work as he apparently heard their footsteps. He immediately broke into a grin and started wiping his hands on a grease rag hanging from an overall pocket.

"Good to see you back," he said to Alex, stepping forward, arm outstretched. "I've been dying to know what happened to the Cessna," he added, his brow creasing. He was a middle-aged guy with a big family, as competent as he was kind and a hell of a mechanic. "I'd just worked on it a couple of days before you took off, remember? And don't think the FAA and every other agency in the country wasn't all over here, looking at my records and books."

Alex introduced Dylan before he explained. "I wasn't feeling very good that day and my memory is shady," Alex admitted. "I recall a sudden drop in the oil pressure, a fire, the engine seizing and the crash. A lot of people are talking sabotage but I don't see how that could be, do you?"

"Did you hear an explosion or something?"

Alex searched his mind. As fuzzy as some things were, he was positive he hadn't. "No."

"Well, I talked to your friend Nate Matthews on the phone. The FBI mentioned him, too, and then there was a lot of talk about that militia group and the way they were staging these horrible shootings on national holidays. You and your buddies were a threat to them, I guess."

"I guess," Alex said.

Tony shook his head. "Memorial Day is coming up—I'm keeping all the kids home. They're throwing a fit because they want to go to the parade with their friends, but I just can't let them do it. We'll go tend my parents' graves like we do every year, but then it's home for movies on the television."

Alex knew Jessica would also go to the cemetery and put flowers on graves of former soldiers and that of her own grandfather, a World War II veteran. It was a tradition in her family, one they had shared over the years. But he hated to hear Tony talk about being afraid for his kids to attend a parade.

"Probably a good idea to stay close to home," Dylan said.

"Yeah," Tony said with a shake of his head. "But kind of sad, too. It's getting so regular folks like me feel they need to carry a gun around."

"Which is exactly the fear these people strive to create," Alex said.

"Yeah. I know, I read that, too." Tony sighed and squared his shoulders. "Okay, give it to me straight. Where is your beautiful Cessna now?"

"Under at least twenty feet of cold lake water. Nate and I are going to dive on it."

"Won't the FAA bring it out of the lake?"

"Yeah, they will. But it's in a remote spot and it's going to take a helicopter and a lot of staging. I want to see it myself before they move it."

"Yeah, I would, too. I'll make a list of things you should look for or check, okay?" Tony offered.

"That's great."

"But that's not why we're really here," Dylan pointed out. He gestured at a few stools pulled up to a workbench. "Let's sit down. We have bad news."

Tony froze in place. "Is it Noreen or one of my children—"

"Nothing like that," Alex rushed to assure him. "It's about Billy."

Tony shook his head. "I know you were looking for him yesterday. He still hasn't shown up? Well, he's late getting here, too. He has a whole bunch of small jobs to perform and it's getting late. When he does get here, I have half a mind to tell him to get lost."

"That won't be necessary," Alex said gently. "We found his body a little while ago. He's been dead since sometime Sunday morning."

Tony sat abruptly. "Dead? How?"

"I'm not entirely sure. On the surface, he was run over at least twice. But it's unclear why he would just lie there and let someone do that to him."

"An accident?" Tony said. "I mean he rode that bike of his everywhere. Did someone run him down beside a road?"

Thinking they wouldn't really know if Billy actually died at the drive-in until all the evidence was analyzed, Alex kept it vague while Dylan didn't respond at all. "It's unclear."

Dylan added, "Do you know if he used drugs?"

Tony looked aghast. "Drugs? I don't think so. They test employees but Billy wasn't really on a formal payroll. I never saw any indications, though."

"How about friends?" Dylan persisted. "Did people come here to see him?"

"Once in a while, but he had trouble with people, you know. He was impressionable and eager to please most of the time, but then he'd get all sullen and quiet."

"You ever see a couple of blond boys about eighteen years old visit him? They're twins so they stand out," Dylan said.

"Blond, good-looking boys?"

"Yeah, I guess you could call them good-looking."

Tony nodded. "I've seen them. They talk to Billy sometimes. Seemed like odd kids for a guy like Billy to know, but they acted friendly enough."

"Billy came by our house Saturday night," Alex said. "I don't think he was aware there was a party."

"Why did he go to your house?" Tony asked, obviously surprised.

"He befriended my wife while I was away. She got to be quite fond of him. But Saturday night he said he came to talk to me. Then he got scared off by all the cops hanging around and claimed he couldn't remember what he wanted. While he was there, I recalled seeing him here on the tarmac the morning I took off. He was deicing a windshield for somebody else, at least that's the impression I got because of the tools he carried. He didn't remember seeing me, though."

"Ordinarily, I wouldn't have remembered one morning out of a hundred, but that morning stands out on account of what happened to you," Tony said. "No one else took off in a private plane that morning and I don't remember Billy being here, either, at least not until later in the day. Now, two days before, that was a different matter. The kid got here early and stayed late, hanging over my shoulder all the time, even refusing to break for lunch."

"Was that unusual behavior for him?" Alex asked.

"Well, sure. It gets a little cold in this hangar in February, you know, so we're all anxious for a few minutes in what we refer to as the lounge. It's that room back there with a table and chairs. Oh, and a heater. It's where we eat our lunch and Billy was as fond of food as the rest of us. But that day, he stayed here, looking at his little cards as though he was trying to remember something."

"Little cards?" Dylan asked, but Alex was pretty sure he knew what Tony was talking about.

"Yeah, you know, those little white cards my

wife puts recipes on, or at least she used to before she got her computer. As long as the directions were real easy, he liked to have them written down."

Alex cleared his throat. "Directions to what?"

"Oh, you know, things like, go get the broom, sweep up garbage, put garbage in can. I don't know what he was looking at that day because it wasn't one of my cards."

"And how do you know that?" Dylan asked.

"Because mine are all pink. They're leftovers from the wife. The one he kept fingering was white."

"What were you working on that day, do you remember?"

Tony shrugged. "Just regular stuff. Engine tune-ups, maintenance checks, you know. It might have been the day I looked at your plane, Alex. Yeah, in fact, I'm sure it was." He frowned for a second. "Sure as heck can't figure out why he'd go to your house at night like that."

"His mother didn't know what he wanted, either. Are you sure he didn't say anything to you about my being back?"

"I haven't seen him since you got back. He didn't come into work Saturday which was unusual for him. The only times he tended not to show up were when he had a problem of some sort he was working through."

"What kind of problem?"

"I don't know, he didn't exactly tell me. I just knew when he was preoccupied. He'd get quieter than ever and go off by himself." Tony sighed as he got to his feet. "The boy had big dreams. I think he was kind of desperate to get away from that house. I gave him rides home when the weather was real bad. His mother was always haranguing him. I don't know how he stood living in that rat's nest."

"I don't, either," Alex said. For the first time, he started wondering about the noise Lynda Summers claimed to have heard in the wee hours of Sunday morning. He'd written it off, but not any longer. Maybe it warranted another look around.

"If you think of anything, let me know," Alex said, and handed Tony a card.

"I will. Damn shame. All and all, I'm going to miss the kid."

"I THINK WE need to talk to the Cummings twins and to Billy's mother sooner rather than later," Alex said.

"Which one first?"

"You go see the twins, I'll go see Lynda Smyth."

"No," Dylan said. "We should stick together."

"I don't think so," Alex said. "Let's drop by the office and talk to the M.E., and then you swing by my house and let me out. I'll get my truck."

"I don't know," Dylan protested. "You heard what the FBI guy said and now Tony is talking about Billy hanging around your plane while it was getting fixed. We stick together."

Alex shook his head. "I'm not budging on this. It's our job to investigate Billy Summers's death and I'm not going to jeopardize what needs to be done so you can hold my hand. Let's stop arguing about it."

"Three months in the mountains didn't cure your stubborn streak, did it?" Dylan said.

"Nope."

By the time Dylan reached Alex's house, they knew that Billy had drugs in his system at the time of death and that he'd been alive when he was run over. There was still no explanation of how he ended up at the old drive-in except that it seemed unlikely he rode there on his bike as there were no discernible bicycle tracks. And if he hadn't ridden the bike, then someone had taken him. Why? Hopefully Billy's mother or the Cummings boys could shed some light on the matter.

"Jessica isn't home yet," Alex said to himself as they pulled in the driveway.

"Did you expect her to be?"

"Kind of."

"Don't worry. She'll be cautious."

"Yeah," Alex said, not at all sure his partner was right. As Dylan roared off, Alex unlocked the garage and got in his truck. It was the first time he'd turned the key in the ignition since coming home, but Jessica had told him she'd run the engine every few days. The truck started right up and he pulled out of the garage.

As he drove away, he attempted to reason with himself. Jessica was fine, she knew he was going to be late, she probably just stopped by a friend's house.

The pep talk grated every raw nerve in his body.

THE LAST TIME Jessica felt like she did today, she'd been eighteen years old and a freshman in college. It had been the first time she'd been away from home and she remembered feeling so excited she could hardly sleep. All the new people and ideas and parties and conversations made her anxious for each new day.

And then things began to change. It started with an uneasy feeling of being watched, causing her to turn while walking across a field or down a hall to see if someone was behind her, looking over her shoulder with uneasy glances. There never seemed to be anyone interested in her and after a few days of it, she began to think she was developing some major psychological problem.

After a week or so of this, she began getting phone calls from a blocked line with no one speaking on the other end. This was followed by someone turning her doorknob in the middle of the night. She considered contacting the campus police but decided against it, unwilling to go public lest her parents be notified. No way did she want them to panic and demand she come home. A few times she managed to yank the door open, but there was never anyone there. When a bouquet of dead flowers greeted her one morning, she decided it was time to enlist the aid of the dorm resident assistant who helped her set a trap.

The perpetrator turned out to be a boy she had in one of her classes. She vaguely remembered that sometime in the first month of school he had hemmed and hawed in an awkward attempt to ask her out. As she wasn't interested in dating him or anyone else at that point, she'd attempted to defuse the request by joking around and making an excuse to rush off. After that, she'd seldom seen him again. And all along, he had been furious with what he thought was her total disregard for his feelings and had decided to retaliate by anonymously stalking her. After she'd apologized up one side and down the other and he had done the same, they'd avoided each other for the rest of term. She wasn't sure what happened to him after that.

And that's how she felt today as she left the Green Mountain Mall. Like someone was watching. It hadn't started until she finished shopping and was making her way back to her car.

In a replay of those long-ago college years, she found herself whipping around to check out the people and cars around her. And as before, she saw no one lurking, nothing threatening.

Alex had asked her to not be alone. She'd thought a mall would be the perfect place to search for a condolence card for Billy's mother. At this hour of the day, the place was crawling with people. But now she realized that there were several ways to be alone and one of the most disturbing ways was to be in a crowd of people you didn't know.

Think about Billy's mother, stop thinking about yourself.

Maybe it was because she was in the process of creating a child that the thought of losing one made Jessica so sick inside. But there was also the fact that Billy had been a generous companion with no agenda of his own except to help her. He'd made her world more beautiful, certainly physically with his gardening, but also figuratively by offering undemanding friendship at a time in her life when that was about all she could handle. And now he was gone.

There was that feeling again. Once more she scanned the immediate vicinity, her eyes peeled for tall, tanned bald men in particular. "There's nothing to be afraid of," she whispered to herself as none materialized, but that wasn't entirely true. The FBI don't warn people for nothing.

Where was all her bravado now? Was someone in this sea of cars staring at her through binoculars?

The inside of the car felt like a real sanctuary and she locked her doors, glad no one could see her acting like a scaredy-cat. All this talk she'd given Alex about not being afraid and here she was frightened of absolutely nothing. She picked up her phone to call him and then remembered what he was doing with his day and put the phone down.

Okay. She would not drive directly home. She would drive the opposite direction to make sure she wasn't being followed. With a plan in mind, she took off, checking her rearview mirror frequently. At first there was the usual crush of traffic on the road leading to and from the mall, but the cars quickly thinned out. At the second red light, a station wagon roared up behind her. She could see inside the car. The two teenage girls in the front seat nodded their heads in time with the radio whose music was loud enough to permeate Jessica's closed windows.

No threat there.

The station wagon turned after a few minutes. Jessica veered off into a fancy neighborhood with narrow streets and little traffic. She meandered around until she realized that not only did she feel totally alone and decidedly unwatched, but that she was behaving like an idiot. She headed home.

A half hour later, she let herself inside the house, dumping her briefcase and purse on the chair. With a sigh, she slipped off her shoes and walked across the room to set the alarm. She stopped suddenly as something caught her peripheral vision. Turning, she gasped, covering her mouth with her hands, unable to move.

ALEX DECIDED THE best chance of engaging Lynda Summers in a candid conversation was to arrive unannounced. After all, the day before, she'd told him she never left the house.

She didn't answer her door and a quick turn of the knob revealed it was locked.

He walked around the yard again just to make sure she wasn't outside somewhere and ended up in back. The big trees stopped most of the rain from falling on his shoulders but it did nothing to stem the stench from the garbage in the lean-to. Once again, the lock on the shed door drew his attention.

Was it possible Lynda Summers had something worth stealing back here?

He walked around the shed, looking for a window and found himself facing a wall of ivy. When he got closer, he could see a window behind the plants and spread the branches a little, getting close enough to peer through the glass while keeping his feet out of the mud in case there were other footprints to be found later.

He could barely make out part of a small room. Shading his eyes from what little glare there was on the glass, the most obvious distinction about the space was how clutter-free it was.

Closest to the window a large model of a red-and-white biplane hung suspended from the ceiling. More or less under that sat a small round table on top of which rested a lamp with a striped black-and-yellow base that brought to mind a bumblebee. A stack of index cards sat next to the lamp. The only other furniture consisted of an old, upholstered chair close to a workbench fronted by a couple of square stools. There were some kind of supplies on the workbench that he couldn't make out.

As Lynda Summers seemed totally incapable of keeping a space this uncluttered, this had to be Billy's hidey-hole. But hadn't she claimed he used the shed as a place to store engine parts?

Alex let the ivy close up behind him and walked back toward the house, determined to get a search warrant. Billy had liked written directions—maybe something on those cards would point to his killer.

Once again he stood on the porch and knocked on the door. Looking through the front window proved fruitless as her junk blocked any view. He took out his cell and phoned her number. Listening closely, he heard a phone ring inside. The woman apparently wasn't home.

He hung up and stood there a second. The phone rang in his hand and he saw Dylan's number flash on the screen.

"I got them," Dylan said, his voice excited.

"Got who?"

"The Cummings twins. I found a piece of torn clothing on their car. It looks like it could have come from Billy's jacket. The whole bumper is a mess like they ran into something. They have no alibi. There are some pills in their glove box, too. I'm taking them in. The lab people and the techs are here. The car will be hauled in pretty soon."

"Wow," Alex said, kind of shocked. "Good work. Did they say how or why they killed him?"

"They say they're innocent. They gave each other alibis that are worth about as much as a three-dollar bill. Listen, I've got to go, partner." He hung up abruptly and Alex did the same.

He needed to go downtown, but first he was going to stop by his house and make sure Jessica had set the alarms. He'd do it sneakylike, so she didn't know he was checking up on her.

Maybe they really had found out who had killed

Billy. But Alex couldn't shake the feeling that even if they had, there was more going on than met the eye....

Chapter Six

Alex did his best to check his temper when he found the front-door alarm had not been set. For that matter, the door wasn't even locked. He knew Jessica was home, because her car was in the driveway. He didn't want to bark at her because she forgot the alarm, but such carelessness coming on top of a day like this one made his nerves twice as jumpy.

"Jessica?" he called. Her things had been dumped on the chair and her shoes sat off to one side. He looked around the room, then called upstairs. "Jess?"

Maybe she was in the kitchen. He started to walk to the dining room when the open patio door caught his eye and he veered that direction.

He found her standing still as death in the yard, rain falling on her head, bare feet buried in the grass. By the looks of her hair, she'd been standing there a while. But it was what was all around her that shook his soul.

Someone had ravaged the garden, butchering every plant and flower with what looked like unbridled rage. A million petals lay on the ground, on the paths, on the grass. Crushed, severed stems bent toward the earth, blossoms trampled into the mud. Limbs had been whacked off bushes, leaving raw, jagged edges. From what he could see, even small branches on trees had been bludgeoned. It looked like a giant whirring blade or an ogre with a vendetta had hacked every living thing. The overwhelming scent of devastated flora permeated the air in a sweet, decaying way that reminded him of a funeral.

Jessica finally registered his presence and turned around to look at him. Her eyes were red, her cheeks tearstained, her lips trembled.

He stood before her and she melted into his arms. Great, silent, heaving sobs shook her body as she cried against his neck and he tried to comfort her. If the maniac who did this appeared right that moment, Alex would have gladly beaten him to a pulp.

"Who would do this to Billy's flowers?" she finally managed to mumble through her tears.

But they weren't really Billy's flowers and that's what alarmed him. This was *their* yard, these were *their* plants. Someone had come through their gate and slaughtered their peace of mind less than twelve hours after the man who had created this beauty was found dead.

"I don't know," he said as he tried to comfort her. "But I'll find out."

JESSICA RAN STEAMING hot water into the tub, lying back to cover her shoulders, closing her eyes, her hands resting on her bare, wet belly.

A mere inch or two away, her baby existed in a liquid world of his or her own. Maybe Alex was right. Maybe she should go to Kansas City and visit her sister.

No, she wouldn't do that. There was a feeling in her bones that something was coming to a head. She was not going to abandon the husband who had just miraculously returned to her no matter how many flowers were torn from their stems.

There was a knock on the door and she called, "Come in."

Alex appeared carrying a mug. "I made you some chamomile tea," he said.

She sat up and accepted the mug. "Thank you. I can't seem to get warm."

"Darn rain," he said, perching on the edge of the tub. "It gets in your bones." She smiled as she took a sip of the tea. They both knew the rain had nothing to do with the chills in her body. "I called a gardening service," he added. "They're coming here tomorrow to clean things up."

"Thank you," she whispered, setting the mug aside. "How was all that destruction accomplished, do you know?"

"Our toolshed was open. The only thing I can find missing is the old machete I stored there for when we went camping, you know, the one with the green cord wound around the handle. Unless you got rid of it while I was…away."

"No," she said, "I didn't move it."

"Might Billy have taken it?" he asked gently.

"I can't see why. I was usually here when he worked and I never saw him touch it."

He nodded and they both fell silent. After a few seconds, she took a deep breath. "I owe you an apology," she said.

"For what?" he asked, his expression puzzled.

"For turning into a zombie when I saw the yard. I left the alarm off, I just froze. But it wasn't only because of the flowers or the thought someone had come into our yard."

"It was because it happened right after Billy's death," he said. "I know."

"Was he murdered, Alex?"

"We think so," he said.

"Tell me about it."

"We know he was alive when he was run over. We know he had drugs in his system, enough to cause his apparent unconsciousness. The M.E.

identified Rohypnol but a complete toxicology will take longer."

"Rohypnol? Isn't that a date rape drug?"

"Yep."

"Good heavens."

"I know. Dylan found torn clothing on the front grill of a car belonging to Ted and Tad Cummings and there is some damage there including a bunch of dents. There were pills in the glove box, he said, and what do you want to bet that they'll turn out to be Rohypnol? The boys aren't talking much, but the techs have the car and the lab is working on the evidence. There was also paint on the bike and the rear bumper reflector is broken. Part of it's missing. They're running tests on that, too."

"Why would the twins fill Billy with a date rape drug and run over him?" she asked, shivering despite the hot water, despite the tea.

"The drug administered in that quantity would have rendered him unconscious and thus compliant. Do you know the twins?"

"They were never in any of my classes, but they were the kind of boys who stood out. Pranks and shenanigans, never anything serious that I knew of. Certainly nothing violent."

He smoothed a lock of damp hair from her forehead. "You're going to hear this from someone, so I'm going to tell you. There are rumors circulating that the Cummings kids were into small-time drugs and they used Billy Summers to collect money and make deliveries."

"I don't believe it," she said.

"I don't know if I do, either."

"And what does any of this have to do with your plane crash, or are we talking about two different things?"

"I think Billy's death and my crash are connected somehow, but I don't know exactly in what way."

"What did Billy's mother say?"

"She wasn't home," he told her.

"Shouldn't you be downtown asking these boys questions?"

"And leave you? Hell, no."

"You have to do your job, Alex."

"Dylan will keep me informed."

"Did you tell him about our yard?"

"Yeah. On the off chance the Cummings twins had anything to do with it I had to."

"It doesn't make sense," she said, shaking her head.

He touched her again as though he couldn't keep his hands from her. The smoldering look in his eyes burned away a layer of cold.

A sigh escaped his lips. "If I stay here much longer, I'm going to jump in and ravage you. I better go make some phone calls."

"Thanks for being honest and up-front with me

about Billy," she said. "I have a very hard time believing anyone would want to harm him." She paused and then added, "I know you're the cop but I have more questions."

"Go ahead and ask them," he said, his gaze lingering on her breasts. "But no promises about the ravaging issue, okay? I may dive in."

She smiled, understanding his banter was tinged with his desire to reassure her that life was normal despite the current situation. She hadn't expected him to refuse to answer any more questions, but she had steeled herself for the old back-off-my-territory tone that used to stop her dead in her tracks. Thankfully, it was absent and that was heartening. "We don't know for certain that your plane was sabotaged, do we?" she began.

"Not for certain, no."

"And we don't know who the contact in Blunt Falls is, you know, the one Agent Struthers told us about."

Alex nodded in agreement, and she continued. "Or if this contact is really interested in you, even if they were before. I mean, I understand trying to stop you last February when you were on your way to help Nate and Mike figure out a conspiracy. But the man behind that portion of this terrorism movement is dead now, so what threat are you?"

"It would have to be because I know the contact

here in Blunt Falls, the person who set me up," Alex said, alarm igniting his eyes. "Is that what you're thinking?"

She nodded. "You're going to keep at this until you figure out what happened to your plane and your friends."

"Is that what you think?" he asked.

The water was growing lukewarm and she shivered. "What do you mean?" she said.

He fixed her with his hazel stare, the one she always thought she'd hate to be on the receiving end of if she had just committed some heinous crime. "My goal is to figure out what happened to protect you and our baby, Jess. And now it's even more important because my gut is telling me Billy was murdered, too, in the here and now, and that it ties back to my plane crash. That means his death is mine to solve, as well."

"How does his death tie to your plane crash?" she asked, wishing she could get out of the water, but she didn't want to interrupt this conversation, so she stayed still.

"I haven't told you about what the airport mechanic said about Billy and the plane," he said. "What with the garden and everything, I completely forgot about it for a while."

"What did he say?"

"He said Billy missed work Saturday, which was atypical. So, the first day it's in the paper that

I'm home, the kid doesn't go to work. Tony Machi said Billy hovered around my plane the day it was serviced. He saw the kid studying index cards, too, and was in fact alone with the plane during a lunch break."

"Was Billy capable of doing something to your plane?"

"Not without help, no. But remember, he was looking at those cards like the ones he asked you to make him so he could tend the garden the way you wanted. And I saw a pile of the same kind of index cards in a shed behind his house."

"I can't believe he would do anything to hurt you."

"You're thinking of the Billy who came to our house and offered you help, who tried to make you happy. But why did he come to help you, and what did he want to tell me the night he showed up here during our party?"

"We need to be certain about the plane," she whispered.

He nodded. "Exactly. If we can prove it was tampered with and that Billy had something to do with it, then that might lead to figuring out who he was in cahoots with. I'll call Nate. As soon as he can get here, I'll borrow a floatplane from John Miter and fly us both up to the lake. I'd better arrange to get hold of some diving equipment, too."

"Who's John Miter?" Jessica asked.

"A guy Dylan and I met out at the airfield last summer," he said.

Last summer—when they hardly spoke to each other. It didn't surprise Jessica that she hadn't heard of this guy.

"Dylan didn't seem to take to John. I, on the other hand, really liked him. He's not the chatty type, but he's definitely got a certain aura about him."

"What do you mean?"

"He lives out on the lake near Crawfish Point in a house he built himself. I know almost nothing about him because he doesn't volunteer information. He's retired now, but he could have been a Superior Court judge, a priest, a mercenary or a crook. When I ask, he just ruffles my hair like I'm ten years old and tells me not to worry about it."

"Sounds interesting but not your normal choice in friends," she said. She shivered from a combination of cold and nerves and asked what she really wanted to know but had been reluctant to broach. "Alex, do you ever worry about piloting again?"

He seemed to think for a moment. "Right after the crash, I swore I was finished with flying. That feeling seems to have faded. I guess I'll know for sure very soon when I take up a floatplane."

"Take me with you," she said softly.

He shook his head adamantly. "No, sweetie. I don't want you anywhere near that lake. We're going to have to find someplace safe for you to stay while I'm gone."

"You're going to find me a babysitter?" she said, irritated. In so many ways he was letting her in, but when he decided to keep her at arm's length it was very hard to get past him. He was doing better, though. He was trying.

He's going to have to try harder and it's obvious that I need to help him.

"Something like that," he said.

"You frustrate me, Alex Foster," she said, casting him an annoyed look. She started to stand and he caught her elbow to steady her.

"I'm sorry," he said.

"I know you're sorry. I'm sorry, too." She stepped out of the tub. "I know you need to go downtown and find out what's really going on. Take me over to Silvia's house. I'll be safe there. The woman has been a principal for eighteen years. Nobody or nothing gets past her."

"Are you sure?"

"Positive."

He handed her a towel and then gently began patting her shoulders dry with another. It brought back memories of their honeymoon, which they'd spent in Hawaii in a very posh place where their room came with a private lanai complete with its own small swimming pool. They'd spent hours in the sun-warmed water, so into each other that the world had almost ceased to exist. What she wouldn't give to zap them both back to that moment in time....

She turned to look at him.

"You're shaking," he said.

"I'm cold."

"I won't let anything happen to you or to me or to our baby. I promise," he said, sliding his hand against her damp skin to rest it on top of her abdomen. His touch made her dizzy and she leaned her forehead against his chest. "Jess? Are you okay?"

She looked up at him with tears in her eyes. "I can't go through losing you again, Alex. Once was enough."

He pulled her closer and claimed her lips.

THE POLICE BUILDING was bustling with activity when Alex arrived after dropping Jessica off at her principal's house. The two women had hugged and Silvia had promised to lock all her doors. They were going to make a quiche for dinner, she said, and Alex was invited to come back and have a piece. He told her he'd do what he could but not to wait for him.

He found Dylan at his desk, finishing up his paperwork. Dylan loved to catch the bad guys, as he put it. He had little patience for lawbreakers of any kind, let alone murderers.

Chief Smyth poked his head out the door and called for Alex and Dylan to join him.

"What have we got?" Smyth asked, seated at his desk. There was a framed photograph of a pretty young woman that caught Alex's attention. The girl had a great smile and a passing resemblance to Jessica.

"My daughter, Stella," Smyth explained. "She's currently away at college."

"She looks like she's a nice kid," Alex said.

"Yes, she is."

"Where does she go to school?"

"Texas," Smyth said, reaching for the crumbled package of cigarettes on his desk. He knew as well as anyone the laws prohibiting smoking indoors in places of employment and Alex knew he wouldn't actually light one up, but the instinct to do so was apparently very strong. "Why do you ask?"

The real reason was that with Jess's pregnancy came the longed-for anticipation of having a child. It had just dawned on him that girl or boy, this baby who was yet to be born, would someday fly away. He shrugged and said, "You must miss her. I bet you can remember every moment of her infancy."

Smyth scowled. "I suppose," he said, and then repeated his earlier question. "What have you guys got for me?"

They detailed their day, checking notes to bring the chief up-to-date on where they went, who they spoke to, what they saw. Smyth knew about Billy's death, of course, and Alex watched him carefully when he mentioned Lynda Summers hadn't been at home when he went to speak to her.

"She was at the funeral home making plans for the time when her son's body can be released for burial," he said somberly. "I know because I'm the one who gave her a ride." He paused for a second and ran a hand over his bald head. Alex thought he might be getting ready to explain his connection to Lynda, a story Dylan had already related. He could think of no way to cut Smyth short that wouldn't reveal they'd been talking about him, something Alex was loath to do, but he needn't have worried. The chief simply cleared his throat.

"I need to get a court order," Alex said. "I need to check out the shed at the back of the house. I managed to look through a window today and saw the cards I told you about, the ones Billy liked to help him keep directions clear in his head."

"You won't need a court order," the chief insisted. "Lynda will allow me to search anywhere that's necessary. I'll meet you there tomorrow, say 8 a.m.?"

"Why not now?" Alex asked. "There are questions about Billy's activities that she needs to answer."

"Because right now, she is under sedation, doctor's orders."

"Did you happen to ask her if she knew anything about Billy being mixed up with drugs in any capacity?" Alex asked.

"By the time I saw her, I knew about the rumors. They spread really fast on this one. Anyway, I did ask her about the Cummings boys and she said they had come around occasionally, she wasn't sure why."

"What about drugs?" Dylan said.

"She said he might have experimented around a little like a lot of guys his age do but that someone would have had to help him procure them because she didn't think he could do it on his own."

"Do you think that's true?" Alex asked.

"Hell, I guess. She seems to underestimate him, though." He sat back in his chair.

"Jessica is going to want to know if Lynda needs help with her son's burial," Alex said.

"She mentioned they have adjoining sites at the cemetery that have been in her family for years. Now tell me what the Cummings boys are saying," Smyth added. The creaking of the leather made Alex wish he could sit down, but he was too anxious to relax.

Dylan perched on a chair, twisting in a way that suggested he'd hurt his back. The guy needed to lay off the gym equipment for a while. "Alex was detained so Kit Anderson joined me in the interrogation room," he began. "Basically, the boys say they were together almost all of Saturday and Sunday. However, their parents were out of town. Tad says they went to a party Saturday night but didn't stay long. They said they walked and that they talked to two girls outside the drugstore. We're trying to find the girls now. And they both maintain that the car they use to go fool around at the drive-in theater was parked in the far back of the acre their parents own and must have been used by somebody else."

"Did they give the key to somebody else?" Alex asked.

"No. But they claim they leave the key in the ignition at all times and all their friends know about it."

"Is that where you found it?" Alex persisted. "In the ignition like they said?"

"Yeah, I did."

"The M.E. couldn't find any traces of blood," Smyth said, pausing as he now fingered a cigarette lighter with a carved silver metal case. "He was able to match the fibers in the grill to Billy's jacket, though, and the pills in the glove box were Rohypnol, the same as found in Billy's bloodstream. Oh, and there were weeds in the tires consistent with those growing at the drive-in lot."

"Did they test the soil underneath the car?" Alex asked. "It sat out in the rain most of the morning.

If there was blood on it, it might have washed off into the soil."

"They didn't find anything."

"What about prints?"

"There are a hundred of them. Every kid in this county must have been in that car at one point or another."

Alex shook his head. "Why would those boys drug and kill Billy? How did they get him out to the drive-in? Are the techs checking the car for evidence Billy was ever in it or that his bike was?"

"They admitted they'd given Billy a ride or two in the past," Dylan said. "Unless we find blood or something, they've got that angle covered. His DNA could have been left behind at any time."

"Is the car big enough to carry the bike?" Smyth asked.

"It would fit in the trunk, but they said they stuffed it in there once when Billy got a flat," Dylan said. "And as for the weeds in their tires, that's tricky, too, because they admit they drive out there sometimes. Hell, I kicked them out myself. What I think is that they arranged to meet Billy at the drive-in to exchange money Billy picked up for them. Maybe they argued, maybe Billy wanted out or threatened to talk if he didn't get a bigger cut. Maybe that's why he really wanted to see Alex, to ask for help with them. Anyway, I think they all did some drugs, and then the twins spiked a soft drink or something with the Rohypnol, then Billy fell into a dead sleep and they either accidentally ran him over or did it on purpose."

"You don't accidentally run over a man Billy's size more than once," Chief Smyth said.

"We have to break their alibi or get them to own up."

"Before their lawyer got there they talked a little. Thank goodness they're over eighteen. They admitted they knew Billy, in fact, they tried to make it sound like they kind of looked out after him and that they even did him favors. They admitted they'd been out to the airport but that was because they liked planes." Dylan straightened his back and sighed. "They didn't give much in the interrogation room even when Kit got a little hot under the collar. Billy Summers is the first body Kit has actually come across and he's taking it kind of hard."

All three men thought about that for a moment.

"Dylan told me your yard was vandalized," the chief finally said, turning his attention to Alex after casting the cigarette pack another longing look. "I suppose we should launch an investigation into that. I'd rather not include the media, however."

"I agree about the media," Alex said. "This has been very traumatic for Jessica. I don't want her subjected to that kind of attention. I also think we can forgo a formal investigation, as well."

"But you guys could be in terrible danger," Dylan said softly.

"I know. I talked to my neighbors before I came in tonight. But you know how the back gate sits out of sight from the street. No one saw anything. And the yard itself was trampled and muddy because of the rain. I checked for a good footprint and couldn't find a single one."

"What kind of tool did the creep use?" Dylan asked.

He told them about the missing machete. "Which would suggest the crime was one of opportunity and not premeditated."

"Are you sure the machete is missing?" Smyth asked.

"Positive. There have got to be easier tools to wield than an old machete but it's about the only thing that would cut plants fast and quietly that was available in the toolshed."

"The question is whether this has to do with the perceived threat the FBI mentioned or is it related to Billy's death," the chief said.

Or both, Alex thought and almost said.

But he didn't.

The conversation he and Jessica had engaged in earlier played through his mind. It was possible someone he knew was behind all or part of this. He looked at Chief Smyth and Dylan, thought about Kit Anderson and Tony Machi….

It just didn't seem possible.

Chapter Seven

Jessica wound up at the school early in the morning because Alex was determined to follow her to work and watch over her until she was safely inside the building and he had an early appointment. He kissed her goodbye, and she watched him drive away through her window.

She knew he was headed out to Lynda Summers's house and that Dylan and Chief Smyth were going to join him. She was glad he wouldn't be alone and she was glad when her class began to fill with students so that she wasn't alone.

She'd taken one last look out at the yard that morning. The devastation seemed worse even though the rain had let up. She wasn't sure what a yard crew could do and she didn't know if she was up to replanting. Alex said he was going to install a lock on the gate, which seemed like a wise precaution.

As the shock of finding the vandalism on the heels of hearing about Billy's death began to wear off, other considerations pushed their way into her consciousness. They'd had a trespasser who had systematically destroyed the sanctuary of their home. Why?

ALEX, CHIEF SMYTH and Dylan arrived in three different cars from three different locations. What was incredible to Alex was that they all arrived at just about the same time.

"Thank goodness the rain let up," the chief said as he got out of his car.

Dylan and Alex joined him on the porch and Smyth knocked. When after several seconds no one answered, Dylan tried looking in the window. Since Alex had taken that route the day before, he knew his partner wouldn't be able to see inside. That's why he was shocked when Dylan said, "It doesn't look like anyone is home."

Alex shifted position and looked in the window. The boxes that had blocked the view the day before were gone.

"Did she know we were coming?" Dylan asked.

Smyth spoke up. "I called her last night and said we needed to ask her some questions and take a look in her shed. She was groggy but I thought she understood me. She mentioned she'd leave the door open in case she nodded off this morning and didn't hear us." He tried the knob and it turned in his hand.

He pushed the door open and called her name. "Lynda?"

Upon entering, Alex turned toward the window that looked out on the porch. The boxes that had towered over the chairs and blocked the window the day before were now in a heap, covering most of the loveseat and big chair. The floor lamp had disappeared completely under the rubble and the television had flown from its table top perch. It lay screen-side down, covered with cable and electrical wires that had ripped from the wall like severed arteries.

But what caught Alex's attention was the sight of a dirty white slipper sticking out from beneath the most ponderous pile of junk. He moved closer until he was sure, and then he began climbing over things, sliding on the trash in his haste. "Over here," he said. "Hurry, she's under all this stuff."

Dylan moved fast, joining Alex, both of them breathing heavily in their attempt to lift the cumbersome boxes off the chairs and free the woman who must be beneath. Smyth shouted cautionary warnings about causing another avalanche. The boxes were unwieldy, weighty with clothing and books, and so old many tore as Dylan tried to pick them up. Their contents spilled everywhere creating more obstacles and mess. All the commotion dislodged the one sure sign Lynda Summers lay under it all, the slipper, which fell to the cluttered floor, revealing a pale foot with bright pink nail polish.

Desperate now but cautious lest they inflict more damage, they moved aside enough rubbish to finally glimpse Lynda. She was dressed in black pants and a pink blouse. Her eyes were closed, her mouth slack and all three men knew she was dead before Alex laid his fingers against her throat to feel for a pulse. He looked over his shoulder and met Chief Smyth's stricken gaze as he shook his head.

It looked as though Lynda Summers's possessions had finally won the battle for her house.

JESSICA WAS IN the process of digging a piece of fruit for a midmorning snack from her lunch bag when the principal, Silvia Greenspan, appeared in her classroom doorway. "You got a call," she began, and for one second, Jessica's heart rate tripled. A statement like that one would have sent her into a tailspin a few days earlier. She set a banana aside and stood up because the expression on Silvia's face finally got through.

"What's wrong?" she asked. "Who called?"

"The emergency room over at the hospital," Silvia said. "They want you to come quickly. Alex has been hurt."

Jessica stood there for a second, trying to take this in, and then she grabbed her sweater off the back of the chair and dug her purse from the drawer. "Did they say how he was hurt or how bad it was?"

"A car accident out on that twisty road north of town."

"Blue Point?"

"Yes, that's it. Connie took the call, but I wanted to tell you myself after last night and everything." By now they were rushing down the hall. "Let me drive you over," Silvia said. "Give me five minutes to cancel an appointment—"

"I'm sorry, I can't wait," Jessica said. Blue Point was the road that led out to Lynda Summers's house.

"Then I'll follow you in a few minutes."

"Fine," Jessica called as she hurried outside. Thanks to Alex's protective streak, and the early time she'd arrived at the school, she had a great parking spot in the front instead of out in the back as usual.

The drive to the hospital was harrowing as her mind raced over the details of Blue Point Road. Had he been hit by another car or had he tumbled over the side into the gorge below? Was he still alive or was she driving to face another nightmare? If someone had hurt him, how would she find that person, because she knew in her heart that she would have to, not only to avenge Alex but to protect herself and thus her child. Had she really told Alex she wasn't frightened for herself? What a load of bunk that was. She was terrified for all three of them.

She parked as close to the emergency-room door as possible and walked inside, mindful to pace herself. All this stress couldn't be good for her baby, she reasoned, plus she was never far from remembering the miracle of being pregnant.

The doctor had told her to be reasonable but to live normally. What was normal anymore? Friends being murdered, vandals, trespassers, terrorists? Okay, so her body had so far cooperated in a way she'd never dreamed it could. Did that mean she should heap more punishment upon it? There was so much at stake.

This pregnancy just had to work out.

The emergency room was crowded with people in various states of trauma, all rushing about. What appeared to be several couples stood clutching each other, their faces stricken with fear as though awaiting to hear the fate of a loved one. Others held small children in their arms while older kids clustered around them, some with cuts and scrapes. Why were there so many children here on a school day?

Jessica stood in a short line until it was her turn to talk to a harried-looking man seated on the other side of the glass window. "I'm looking for Alex Foster," she said, scanning the room, keeping her eyes open for a sign of Dylan or Chief Smyth, both of whom she knew Alex had been meeting with that morning.

"Was he on the bus?" the receptionist asked.

"The bus? What bus?"

"The school bus," he said, and answered a phone, motioning with his finger for her to wait. Then he began digging through papers, apparently to look up something for whoever was on the other end of the phone.

Jessica leaned forward. "What bus are you talking about? Alex Foster is my husband. I got word from you that he was injured in a vehicle accident. He's a police detective—"

The man was completely ignoring her, and she turned away. There had to be someone else who could help. Had Alex collided with a school bus, was that what was going on? She saw a nurse talking to one of the worried-looking couples and approached, waiting as patiently as she could while the nurse directed them toward metal doors.

"Excuse me," she said as the couple hurried off. The nurse turned to face her and Jessica could see in her eyes that she only had a few seconds to explain things. "I'm looking for my husband," she began, and gave an abbreviated version of what she wanted.

The nurse scanned the clipboard she held in one hand. "I don't see his name. When did he come in?"

"I don't know. I received the call about thirty minutes ago."

"Was he on the Mountain View school bus?"

"I don't think so. Was there an accident?"

"A bus full of kids on their way to a holiday program overturned while rounding a sharp curve on a highway ramp," the woman said.

"Out on Blue Point?"

"No, over by Campton."

Jessica's mind could not wrap itself around what she was hearing. Campton was fifteen miles north of Blunt Falls. What was Alex doing way over there?

"What kind of holiday program?" Jessica asked, suddenly remembering Memorial Day was only five days away.

"I'm not sure. Anyway, they sent us the overflow because the Campton hospital is so small. Maybe he's over there."

"Who would I ask to find out?"

"Wait right here. I'll look around in the back to see if he's in a treatment room and then call Campton. His name is Alex Foster, right?"

"Yes."

"Why don't you sit down," the nurse said kindly. "I won't be long."

There was suddenly someone at Jessica's elbow and she turned, hoping to find Alex. Silvia had arrived and now stood beside her. She took Jessica's arm. "She's right, you should sit down."

Jessica swore under her breath as she retrieved her cell phone. "I'll try calling him," she said. "If he's stuck in a treatment room somewhere, maybe he'll answer."

She punched in his number and he picked up before the ring stopped. "This is Alex," he said.

"Alex!" Jessica closed her eyes for a second. At least he was able to hold a phone and talk. How badly could he be hurt?

"Are you okay?" she asked.

"I'm a little busy," he said. "Is anything wrong?"

"I got a call you were in the emergency room, that you'd been in an accident. Are you telling me you haven't?"

"Who called you?" he demanded.

Jessica tried to explain, and then Silvia got on the phone and told Alex about the call. Jessica sank down on a chair, weak now that the adrenaline rush had spent itself. When the nurse reappeared shaking her head, she told her there'd been a mix-up.

But had there really been a mix-up or had this been a deliberate ruse to—to what? What had been accomplished except scaring the daylights out of her? Did it have anything to do with the busful of children?

Silvia handed her back the phone. "Are you going back to the school?" Alex asked.

"I guess."

"Good. It's disturbing that whoever sent you on that wild-goose chase knew I'd be out on Blue Point. Go home with Silvia, okay? I have to finish something up here and then I'll come for you at her house."

"Okay. And you'd better call the Campton police and tell them to make sure that school-bus accident was really an accident."

Chapter Eight

As soon as Alex got off the phone with the Campton police, Dylan joined him in the one small clear spot they could find in the cluttered room.

"Everything okay with Jess?" he asked.

For some reason, Alex was reluctant to talk about what had happened until he could investigate it a little on his own. "Fine," he said.

Dylan nodded curtly. He held up a prescription-pill bottle by lifting the plastic bag in which it had been deposited. A few capsules rattled around inside it. "Kit found this near her body," he said.

"Are you familiar with them?" Alex asked.

"Yeah. They're a damn strong tranquilizer. Her doctor prescribed them yesterday," Dylan said. "Five of the ten are gone, which is pretty potent. I wonder if Chief Smyth took her to pick them up."

Alex shook his head.

"Anyway," Dylan continued, "if she'd taken a couple of these and gone to sleep, the whole house could have landed on her head and it wouldn't have roused her."

"Why did the boxes fall if she was asleep and not moving?" Alex mused aloud.

"Maybe her recliner hit them."

"Did Kit find a glass of water in there with her?"

"Not yet. But he's not finished."

"Her son was murdered two days ago," Alex said. "That's why I want her checked for anything suspicious. Make sure you bag her hands," he called to Kit Anderson, who cast him a look that clearly said, *Don't tell me how to do my job.* Buck up, Kit, Alex thought. He wanted to make sure she had died exactly the way it appeared she'd died, and that meant there wasn't any DNA under her fingernails where she'd scratched an attacker or defensive wounds on her hands or arms where she'd fended someone off.

"Where is the chief?" Alex asked.

"He wandered off a while ago," Dylan said, twisting around and stretching his well-built frame.

Alex recalled seeing him do the same thing the night before in Smyth's office, though he sure hadn't spared any effort uncovering Lynda Summers's body. "What's the matter," he joked. "Did you pull something when you were picking up cars or whatever it is you do to buff that physique?"

"I lift weights, dummy," Dylan said with a smile. "You ought to try it sometime. The girls think it's sexy as hell."

"Hmm—I'm going to go find Smyth."

One of the paramedics overheard him and hollered he'd seen Smyth go outside. Alex walked out the front door, anxious to drive to the school and see Jessica with his own eyes.

Why had someone pulled such a stupid prank on her? He could see no purpose in it. He planned to question the woman who had taken the call and see if the incoming number had registered on the phone. He was willing to bet that would be a dead end. Was this prank related to Billy's death and the vandalized flowers? It all seemed like a disjointed mishmash.

He found the chief inside the shed, standing near the striped lamp. Smyth apparently heard him approach for he turned around, his expression startled. "The door was unlocked," he said.

"The lock was in place when I was here yesterday," Alex said, glancing at the hasp.

Smyth rubbed his chin. "Lynda must have come out here and opened it before she fell asleep last night," he commented. His voice held notes of regret, though the tears that had moistened them briefly were long since gone.

"Did you hurt yourself?" Alex asked when he

noticed angry red scratches on the back of the chief's right hand.

The chief immediately stuck his hand in his pocket. "My daughter's cat. Of course she couldn't take him to Texas with her and he hates me. It's nothing. Long as we're here, we might as well take a look."

"Sounds good to me," Alex said, glad to finally get a chance to look around. An extension cord had been strung to connect the lamp to electricity. He switched on the light and immediately looked for the three-by-five index cards he'd glimpsed the day before. They were right where he'd seen them. Using the eraser end of a pencil, he turned the top one so he could read it.

"What's it say?" the chief asked.

"It's directions for planting rosebushes," Alex told him. "This is Jessica's handwriting."

The chief grunted. "Did you see the paper this morning?"

"No, as a matter of fact, I didn't. We were running late."

"There's a blurb in there about your garden being vandalized. I thought we agreed to keep it out of the news."

"We did," Alex said. "I mean, I didn't alert the newspaper."

"Maybe your wife—"

"Absolutely not. No way."

Smyth shook his head. "What's on the next card?"

Alex glanced at the cards in order. All of them held gardening notes except for the pink one on the bottom which gave simple directions for blocking the wheels on a plane. The handwriting on this one must belong to Tony Machi.

"There's nothing important in these cards," Alex said, disappointed. But hadn't the stack been higher yesterday? He searched his memory, trying to recall what had made him think there were well over a dozen cards instead of six or seven.

"I didn't know the kid had the place set up like this," the chief said as he stared around the room.

"It's nice," Alex said. He glanced at the workbench that held paints, glues and pieces of wood along with model airplane boxes. The resulting airplanes Billy had apparently built from the kits were clumsy and heavy-handed, but there were several lined up on a shelf as though he truly enjoyed his hobby.

"First your beautiful garden and now this," Smyth said quietly.

Alex could see no sign of destruction in the shed and wondered to what the chief was alluding until it finally dawned on him that he wasn't referring to the negative energy of vandalism but to the creative aspects of Billy's interests. "He was a man of surprises," Alex said. Had they misjudged him? Was he really a lot brighter than everyone gave him credit for?

But the models weren't without faults and were obviously the work of someone challenged to paint and glue without making mistakes.

"Look at this one," the chief said, gazing up at the big biplane hanging in front of the window.

This plane was different from the others. Not only larger, but the design came complete with details the others lacked and superior overall workmanship. Red paint glistened on the fuselage, while the propeller looked as though it would spin easily if it had been low enough to the floor for Alex to reach it.

"There you guys are," Dylan called from the doorway. He whistled long and low as he looked around. "Wow. This place is a little oasis of calm in a sea of chaos, isn't it?"

"Yeah, it is," Smyth said, looking around. He sighed deeply as he appeared to absorb the details of the small room. "Who would have guessed the boy had it in him?"

AFTER SMYTH SENT Dylan to Campton to check out the bus accident, Alex drove to the Cummingses' house. He'd learned the twins hadn't been arrested, although the D.A. was considering an investigation. He had no plans to talk to them; he just wanted to get a feeling for the lay of the land.

He slowed down his truck and looked at the property. It was easy to see where they must have parked their joyriding car because of the tracks made by the tow vehicle that had taken it into the police-compound yard the day before. And from what Alex could tell, no one would see that car from the house due to the placement of a large barn between them. It was possible somebody else had taken it unobserved.

He got out of the truck and stared at the house for a minute. It had obviously once been a farm of some kind with a two-story house and a covered porch. It needed a new coat of paint, but things were relatively well kept. He was walking back to his truck when someone called out to him. He turned to see two blond young men coming toward him.

"You lost or something, mister?" one of them asked as they both leaned against the fence.

Alex introduced himself and told them who he was.

"We aren't talking to you," the other one said. "Mom and Dad are at work and they told us not to talk to anyone. Besides, you guys don't listen. We don't know how Billy's clothes got caught in our grill. And it's all banged up because it's a drag car. It's been banged up forever. I don't know when every single dent got made and I don't know how those pills got in our glove box."

Alex looked at them closely. "You guys were friends with Billy?"

"Sure," they said in tandem.

"Billy was okay," the shorter one added.

Alex couldn't think of a single question to ask them that wouldn't be better asked downtown with a recorder playing, so he said nothing. His silence apparently goaded them on.

"He wasn't like other guys," the taller one said. He stuck out a hand and added, "I'm Tad, that's Ted. You're a lot cooler than the psycho body-builder who came out here. We used to look out for Billy in school. He was a couple of years older than us, but not older in his head, you know?"

Alex nodded.

"And he didn't do drugs," Ted added. "Okay, sometimes Tad and me dabble a little—nothing hard-core, just weed—but we'd never involve Billy. We were teaching him how to build model airplanes and he was getting pretty good."

"You made the red-and-white biplane in Billy's shed, didn't you?"

Tad smiled. "You've seen it? Yeah, we did that. Well, mostly Ted, but I helped. We let Billy do some of it, too, but he got all upset when we started detailing it in a way that wasn't in the directions."

"Billy liked to follow the rules," Ted said. "Coloring outside the lines made him nervous."

"Well, the model turned out great," Alex said.

"Thanks. I want to ask his mom if we can have it, you know, to remember him and stuff. Do you think she'd mind?"

"I'm sorry to have to tell you that Lynda Summers is dead," Alex said. It would be all over town soon enough.

"How?"

"Some of her belongings apparently toppled over and crushed her," Alex said.

"Oh, man, that's tough," Tad said. "Both her and Billy, huh? That's terrible."

"Funny thing about Billy," Ted chimed in. "He didn't want his mom to know about the shop we kind of created out behind the house. He was afraid she'd take it over."

"Probably a valid concern," Alex said. He knew the D.A.'s office would blow a gasket if he kept talking to these guys, but he was glad he'd had the chance to meet them. They seemed like pretty decent people to him and too straightforward to be killers. Still, you never knew.

"I have to be getting along," he said. "My wife is expecting me." He watched them both to see if they exchanged knowing looks, but Tad just smiled. "That's why your name is familiar. Your wife is the lady Billy was helping in the garden, right? And you're the guy those jerks at B-Strong tried to kill. You were in the paper."

"My claim to fame," Alex said.

A minute later, he drove away. In the rearview mirror he watched Tad and Ted turn back toward their house. He honestly didn't know if he'd just been conned or not.

ALEX AND JESSICA drove to the airport to pick up Nate that evening. Alex had met her at Silvia's a while ago and they hadn't been apart since then.

Three days ago, both of the Summerses had been alive and well, and now both were dead. It was unbelievable. "Do you think Lynda's death was an accident?" she asked Alex.

He shrugged. "I'm not sure. I'm treating it like a homicide until I am."

She pressed his leg and smiled when he looked over at her. "I want you to know that I've arranged to spend the evening with Silvia tomorrow. When you and Nate get home from the lake, call me and I'll meet you at the house."

"I have a better idea," he said, throwing her a longer glance, this one accompanied by a grin. "Come with us."

"I thought you didn't want me near your lake."

Another shrug. "I just want to have you close by. You don't have to come—"

"I'd love to come," she said. "Will Nate mind?"

"Of course not. It might be kind of boring, though."

She laughed. "If you can spend three months up there alone, I think I can handle three hours. Did you get a chance to ask Tony what to look for?"

"Yeah. He gave me some ideas. Nate got permission from the FAA to dive as long as we buoy the location for them to take a look at later. It's understood we won't remove anything from the plane."

"And the float plane is ready to go?"

"And loaded with dive gear." He frowned as he said, "I'm not telling anyone where or even that we're going anywhere and I'd appreciate it if you did the same." He paused and added, "Did you mention it to Silvia?"

"No," she said, "and that's weird because why wouldn't I? I just didn't. You're not telling anyone at work?"

"No."

"Do you think one of them had something to do with the crash?"

"Of course not, but people talk. Just look at Dylan and his continual effort to impress young women."

"Like his new car?"

"I haven't seen it yet. Some eighteen-year-old in Billings got it rear-ended, so it's in a shop."

"I bet that's the end of that romance," Jessica said.

"Yeah." Alex laughed. "He's incorrigible. Anyway, I'd just as soon not everyone in town knows what we're doing. I just want to check this out without arousing too much curiosity, so I'm borrowing everything we'll need from the guy I told you about."

"John Miter."

"Yeah. We'll leave from his place, not the Blunt Falls airport. I'll just call in sick." He shook his head. "I have to ask you. Did you talk to anyone from the press about our garden disaster? It was apparently in the paper."

"Of course not," she said. "Really, it was in there? That's news? Probably because you're just back home."

"I know," he agreed. "Dylan pointed out the chief himself talks to his pet reporter all the time. He probably let something slip. He does like publicity and he does talk."

"Yeah, he does," she said. "I think we should stop getting that newspaper."

NATE WAS WALKING through the door as they pulled up in front of the terminal. Montana always sported its share of rugged men in boots and Stetsons, but Nate still stood out. There was just something magnetic about his laid-back personality that shone through. Tonight, he carried a satchel in one hand but his other was wrapped around that of a tall woman with black hair and clear blue eyes.

"Who is that?" Alex said.

"I think that's Mike Donovan's daughter, Sarah. Didn't Nate tell you he and she got together while trying to figure out who killed her dad?"

"He hinted around but nothing definite. Guess he wanted to show, not tell," Alex said as he pulled to a stop. "She's sure a heck of a lot prettier than Mike."

Jessica knew that after her father's murder, Sarah and Nate had spent a few very intense days together outwitting a determined killer. And in that time, according to Nate, they'd fallen in love. Since then, Sarah had moved to Arizona to be near Nate and started veterinarian school to fulfill a lifelong dream.

The two of them slid into the backseat, so obviously in love that it made Jessica smile. She'd never seen Nate like this, never seen his eyes dance and his lips twist into a smile every time someone spoke. "I brought my girl," Nate said as they all shook hands across the seat backs.

"I tried to get him to warn you," Sarah said, directing her comment to both Jessica and Alex. "He wanted me to be a surprise. I hope I'm not a terrible inconvenience."

"Of course you aren't," Jessica said warmly. "I'm delighted I'll have some company while these two dive on the plane. Unless you're also a diver, of course, and plan to go down with them."

"I'm not a diver but when Nate asked if I wanted to come, I jumped at the chance," she explained. "I've heard an awful lot about that lake. I want to see it with my own eyes."

"You and me both," Nate said. He gazed at Jessica for a moment and added, "You look absolutely beautiful. Pending motherhood agrees with you."

She smiled her thanks.

For Jessica, the ride back to the house along with sitting around the table and discussing plans for the next day while eating take-out Chinese food were some of the nicest times she'd had in recent memory. When their marriage began to come apart at the seams, they'd stopped socializing as a couple. She'd forgotten how charming Alex could be when he was relaxed and comfortable, and not having other Blunt Falls police officers around to talk shop with was kind of refreshing.

Not that Nate didn't talk law enforcement. He was a deputy, after all, and he'd been doing that as long as Alex had been in the police department. What they spoke about tonight, however, was pertinent to all of them because they'd all been touched by the delusional madness of the Shatterhorn man with the warped agenda.

And they'd all been left with the knowledge that

it wasn't over, that their bad guy wasn't the only crackpot around.

Alex told them about the former employee of the Shatterhorn Killer who had reportedly called a suspect in Seattle about another case and mentioned Blunt Falls in the conversation. "Agent Struthers thinks the reference ties back to someone here in town who was involved with my plane crash," he concluded.

"Any idea who?"

"None."

"Who was this guy?"

"We were given the alias he used in Nevada. William Tucker, sixtyish, tanned, bald. Cold eyes. Do you want to see a photo?"

"Sure," Nate said.

Alex stood and started off to the den. "I'm not sure why this guy would bother coming after me, though. I'm no longer a threat."

"Someone thinks you are," Nate called after Alex, who soon returned with the photo in hand. "Here. Ever seen him?"

Nate nodded. "Once, but not in person and not tanned like this. I saw him on a closed-circuit screen over an intercom. I wondered what happened to him after his boss was hit and killed by that car. I even wondered if this guy was behind the wheel."

Sarah had gotten to her feet and come to take a look. "I don't recognize him," she said.

"You didn't get out of the car, you never saw him," Nate said. He turned his attention back to Alex. "I take it neither of you has seen this guy around here?"

"Not a glimpse," Alex said.

Eventually the conversation led to the events of the past few days. Nate was as baffled as Alex and Jessica by the purpose of the bogus call from the emergency room. This was the first time Jessica thought to ask Alex if he'd heard back from the Campton police—was the school-bus accident really an accident?

"Dylan drove over there and talked to them face-to-face," Alex said. "He came away with the impression there isn't a doubt in the world it was an accident. Children have been targeted before by these kinds of domestic militia terrorist groups, but not like this. Plus the bus was overdue for maintenance and one anonymous source told him the front tire was almost bald. They checked out the driver, too. She's the mother of six and she's been driving for the school district for years."

"But what about the holiday program the nurse mentioned?"

"It was an end-of-the-school-year picnic event at a park."

"You have to ask yourself," Nate said, sitting

back in his chair and stretching his long legs, "if the only thing accomplished was frightening Jessica—was that the purpose?"

"But why me?" Jessica murmured. "I'm no threat."

"Maybe you're not a threat, but you *are* the most important person in the world to a man who is," Nate said, looking right at Alex and then back at Jessica. "Your flowers, your husband—your peace of mind. It's certainly affecting how you feel and hence, how Alex feels."

Alex took Jessica's hand in his and squeezed it.

"One more thing that's been bothering me," Nate said, sitting forward and resting his weight on his forearms. "Whenever you describe the plane crash, you get real fuzzy on details."

"I've noticed that, too," Jessica said. "I thought it might be because he hit his head in the crash."

"He had the wherewithal to exit the plane and save his life," Nate said. "And just because he suffered a few cuts doesn't mean he hit his head."

"I don't think I did," Alex said, unconsciously, it seemed, touching the scars on his face.

"It's the time before the crash that you seem vague about," Nate added. "Why is that?"

Alex paused to think for a moment. "I have no idea. I remember being in a funk. It must be that."

"A funk?"

"Yeah, you know."

Jessica looked Nate in the eye. "He means we'd had a big old, hairy argument before he left. We were both in a funk."

They all kind of looked at each other uneasily, and then Nate chuckled. "That occasionally happens to everyone," he said. "Come on, Alex, why don't you and I clean up."

While the guys performed domestic chores, Jessica led Sarah out into the yard. She turned on the floodlights so they could look around.

"It doesn't look too bad," Sarah said diplomatically.

And in a way, she was right. The yard crew had removed the shattered stems and ruined blossoms, pruning things back, remulching the paths and toting away debris until now the yard looked wooded and serene in its way. But it wasn't the riot of color it had been and Jessica could barely stand to look at it.

"I'm sorry about your friend," Sarah added.

"Thank you. He was a nice kid." Jessica waited a second and added, "It appears Nate recovered from the bullet wound okay. Is he 100 percent now?"

"Yes. The doctors were amazed how quickly he healed." She hugged herself and shivered. "Jess, I don't mind telling you. I thought he was going to die."

"It must have been terrible," Jessica said.

Sarah nodded. "That's really why I came. I couldn't bear to have him involved in this situation without me. My coming means we have to leave late tomorrow afternoon because I have a big exam the next day, but it was worth it."

"I totally understand," Jessica said. She liked Sarah, and that was an unexpected treat, too. Nate's last girlfriend had been something of a prima donna with a grating laugh and though Jessica had tried to be friendly, they just hadn't clicked. "Are you planning on having children eventually?" she asked, then shook her head. "Never mind. That's none of my business. I guess I have babies on the brain."

"I don't mind," Sarah said, smiling deeply. "I can't think of anything we want more than a family. My own youth was dominated by an addictive mother and a father I could never seem to get close to. Children will be my chance to experience childhood again, this time through a better lens. I want to finish school first, though, and even though it seems incredible to me, Nate and I have only been together three months. We're still finding things out about each other." A frown furrowed her smooth brow for a moment, and then she added, "The only thing that blackens the horizon is this lingering threat. And to think that Alex might still be in danger—it's horrible."

"Yes, it is," Jessica whispered.

"Do you think the man who worked on your garden was killed by these people? Was he one of them?"

"No," Jessica said profoundly. "Of course he wasn't. We told you about him. He was a simple guy who seemed to always try to do his best. When he found out I wanted the flowers to put on my grandfather's grave he worked even harder."

Sarah nodded thoughtfully. Then she said, "You must be right about him. There's certainly nothing simple about this situation, is there?"

"There sure isn't," Jessica agreed.

"Maybe tomorrow we'll find some answers," Sarah added.

Jessica nodded but she thought it far more likely they would simply find more questions.

Chapter Nine

They were up before dawn the next day because John Miter's place was twenty miles out of town. It was a quiet, somber drive fueled by nerves, coffee and the inevitable Vita-Drink.

As Alex yawned into his hand, it brought back memories of the day he'd flown off into the blue and not come home for a while. He'd been yawning that day, too. But today the yawns were just yawns. There was no accompanying thirst and lethargy, no mental sluggishness.

If there had been, he would have grounded himself. One crash into that lake was enough for a lifetime.

They took off into a beautiful sunrise and it felt great to soar above the clouds. This was something he hadn't been sure he'd ever do again, but now that he was flying, he knew he wouldn't let fear stop him. He twisted the lid off one of his enhanced waters and encouraged everyone else to join him. "Here's to life," he said, and they clapped the plastic bottles together.

Nate acted as navigator as they flew through the clear blue skies, keeping track of their route on the charts Alex had brought along. Thanks to the FAA, he knew exactly where "his" lake was and sure enough, ninety minutes later, he caught the first glimpse of the river he'd followed to the Bookers' house. From up here, it looked like an easy walk, the gullies and crevices mitigated by height. The truth had been that a two-day walk turned into several times more than that. He'd had to avoid all sorts of hazards including melting snow and the small avalanches that could still be deadly.

And then he caught sight of the lake, a blue gem set in dark green trees, a diamond brooch on an emerald gown. Patches of snow glistened on the peaks of neighboring mountains.

"Is that your lake?" Jessica asked, leaning forward.

He nodded. Then he glanced back at her over his shoulder. "It looked a lot bigger last February."

"Yeah, I bet."

They circled until Nate pointed. "I see the Cessna, over there, not far from the shore."

He was right. The vague but unmistakable shape of the plane was visible beneath the pristine lake water. It had sunk within fifty yards of the shoreline. To Alex, dragging himself across it with a busted leg and during a snowstorm, it had seemed more like fifty miles. And beyond it on the shore, barely visible, he glimpsed the arrow made of rocks that pointed inland toward his camp.

As he'd lugged those rocks into place a few weeks before, he'd imagined it would appear like a beacon to anyone flying over, but in truth, you had to know to look for it—his rocks tended to blend in with all the others. He wished now he'd scattered them before he left. Fact was he'd completely forgotten about them.

He landed into the wind, then steered the plane toward the downed Cessna. Peering into the water and seeing the ghostly white wingspan of his plane down below felt eerily disquieting. This lake, except for some good luck, could easily have been his grave, the Cessna, his tombstone.

And now he was back to a place he'd once planned never to see again.

Nate inflated the dinghy with a CO_2 canister as Alex anchored the plane between the wreck and the shore. When the boat was inflated, Alex ferried Sarah and Jessica to the beach. "I'll go get Nate and our equipment next," he told Jessica, fighting off the urge to ask her not to wander far, to stay where he could see her. Had coming back here spooked him more than he thought it would? Yeah, he decided. Literally, he'd been gone for only five days. But in his head, this place had happened a lifetime ago.

Take that big pine tree right over there. Last winter there had been five feet of snow around it. That was the place he dug out a trench for himself and spent a few miserable nights just fighting to stay alive. A wave of nausea passed through him now, remembering the pain and even more, the hopelessness.

"Where was your camp?" Jessica asked, and he tore his gaze away from the tree.

He waved in a vague direction. "Over there."

"I'd like to see where you lived."

"Where I *live* is in a nice little house with a drop-dead gorgeous woman who is going to have my baby. That's where I live now and that's all that matters."

"Don't be obstinate," she said.

He smiled but he really didn't want to be having this conversation. However, if he didn't compromise, she'd come unglued, so he touched her arm. "If there's time after our dive, I'll give you a personal tour, okay? Or maybe we could just fly over it."

She nodded, her gaze hard to read.

"I'll go get Nate so we can put on our gear."

He faced the floatplane as he rowed the dinghy because he didn't want to see the disappointment on her face. He understood that she wanted to know exactly where and how he'd lived, so why couldn't she understand that it was painful for him? Walking along that trail back to his camp would feel like hiking back to despair. He didn't need to revisit it; he was happy to let it go.

Within an hour, Nate and Alex had changed into wet suits and donned scuba tanks. Pulling the dinghy behind them to tote their gear, they said enthusiastic goodbyes and paddled back out to the wreck. The bright orange buoy they'd attached made finding it from water level a cinch.

"What exactly are we looking for?" Nate said before he bit down on the mouthpiece that would feed air from his tank. With his mask pulled back on the top of his head, his expression was intense. Alex couldn't think of anyone he wanted by his side more than this man.

"Anything to do with the engine and oil pressure. Tony told me to check to make sure the oil-tank plug is in place because of the way the pressure dropped so quickly. He doesn't see how, but maybe it blew. He explained where it is. Hopefully the plane didn't settle with that area in the mud, but the struts broke when I landed so we'll just have to see."

Nate grinned. "You mean when you crashed."

Alex chuckled. "Yeah, well, anyway, thanks to the FAA wanting to make their own assessment, we won't move anything, but we can photograph the hell out of it. Ready?"

In another minute they disappeared below the water, a trail of bubbles marking their spot.

"I'LL BE BACK in a few minutes," Jessica said as soon as she saw Alex and Nate dive beneath the water.

Sarah got to her feet. "Where are you going?" she asked, her head tilted to one side.

Jessica paused, uncertain how to explain. There was no way to sugarcoat it, however, so she just told the truth. "I imagine you've gathered from things you've heard that Alex and I have…struggled. We're just getting back to a place where we can work together, but he still resists. The fact is, just as you had to be here for Nate, I have to be here for Alex even if he doesn't admit it and part of being here is understanding what he's been through. He's so reluctant to talk about it, so anxious to move on. I can't go quite that fast."

"You're going to go look for his camp, aren't you?" Sarah asked.

"Yes. If it were Nate, wouldn't you?"

"In a heartbeat. Do you want company?"

Jessica shook her head. "No, if you don't mind, I'd rather go alone."

"I don't mind," Sarah said. "I'll stay here and

make sure their bubbles keep rising to the surface. Do you know exactly where the camp is?"

"He told me the trail is marked by a forked tree on the lake end. I've been looking around and it seems to me that little fir tree right over there has two crowns. But even if it didn't, there's an arrow of rocks on the beach. Alex must have made that this spring when the snow melted, hoping a plane would see it." She stopped talking abruptly as a lump swelled in her throat. He must have felt so alone.

"Just be careful, okay? If you get eaten by a bear, Alex will kill me," Sarah said as Jessica took off toward the trailhead.

As soon as Jessica passed behind the forked tree, the world seemed to disappear. The plants on the path had worn away and the dirt was rutted. It had probably been an animal trail long before Alex started using it.

As the trees and bushes on either side of it closed in, she imagined Alex stumbling, limping down this path. What would she have done? Looked for a clearing of some kind, but not too far from the lake. The lake meant food and possible rescue.

The clearing was suddenly upon her as she stepped around a bush covered with thorns into a space about ten feet by twelve. A campfire ring sat under an outcropping of rocks, and across from it, branches had been woven together to create a shelter against the edge of a cliff. The trails between the two spaces paused at a trio of large boulders, the camp version, she supposed, of a dining room.

And that was about it.

Oh, there were a few scraps around like fish bones and charred wood stakes he must have used to smoke the fish he carried out with him, even a stack of unburned branches waiting to cook another meal. Half of a small rectangular blue-and-white metal box sat on one rock but it was currently empty. Judging from the rust, she wondered if he'd used it to transport water.

What was lacking were all the things she'd spent her camping experiences taking for granted. The sleeping bags, the tents, the pots and pans, and water jugs. There were no paper products like newspapers or magazines, no dishes of any sort except for a few pieces of bark stacked on one of the rocks that looked as though they may have been used as plates.

She stood there in the utter silence of the day, stunned by the paucity of supplies and stimuli. She sat down on one of the rocks, on a spot that seemed to have a natural place for a human haunch, and felt certain Alex had perched here a hundred times while he cooked his fish and dreamed of coming home.

Had she secretly wondered if he'd really been

up in the mountains for three months? Had his reluctance to talk about the details seemed so over-the-top that she'd imagined he might have made some of this up? And wasn't it odd that glimpsing his plane under the lake and that sad little arrow on the beach wasn't half a gut-wrenching reality check as this camp and its almost exclusive lack of civilization?

After a few minutes, she decided to investigate the other structure that lay kitty-corner to the fire. What she found was a small, cozy sleeping area. The floor was covered with branches topped with a layer of boughs, she supposed for softness. A pair of worn handcrafted crutches constructed from tree limbs and tied with plant fiber leaned against the back wall. Alex had told her he walked out with his backpack, clothes, some food and little else, so there wasn't much there besides what nature could provide. She saw the other half of what she now recognized was the blue-and-white metal medical box the emergency supplies had come in. This half held a handful of what appeared to be cold charcoal pieces from the fire. Hanging from an exposed root above, she found a small array of sticks hanging from a piece of salvaged metal. Additional sticks and cones were tied with plant fiber and dangled from the main structure. She blew on it and the pieces bumped together and made a pleasant sound. He'd made himself a wind chime of sorts.

Unable to resist the temptation to try to understand better, she crawled inside and lay down atop the boughs. It would never take the place of a good mattress, but it wasn't bad. He must have used his coat and additional foliage for more warmth or maybe he'd slept closer to the fire at first when the weather was colder. She laid her head back and saw that he'd left a small opening near the top she could easily picture being filled with stars once night came and she remembered that first night he was home and the way he'd paced endlessly until finally ending up outside, under the stars.

Taking a deep breath she laid her head down and looked up at the ceiling. For the first time, she saw that he'd made marks along one wall with the charcoal, little lines in groups of five no doubt counting off the nights he'd spent in this camp. But it's what she saw next that literally took her breath.

Up above the lines, easily visible from a reclining position, was a drawing. It would never hang in the Louvre, but it brought tears to her eyes as she recognized her own face smiling down at her.

ALEX HAD SPENT weeks watching the snow melt and he knew that a hundred little streams ran into and fed this lake before escaping out the other side into a river that eventually wound its way to the sea. He'd followed that river to safety, back to Jessica and his life.

But now the task at hand was to check out his poor, wounded plane and he was relieved that although the water was icy cold, it was also clear. Visibility was excellent.

The plane had turned a little as it sank, coming to land on the rocky bottom with the fuselage propped on one of several big boulders. This was a stroke of luck as it meant the engine compartment would be accessible. Beside him, Nate pointed at the area behind and beneath the broken propeller and they kicked their way down.

Looking at his wonderful plane as he descended brought back a decade of bittersweet memories. He'd inherited the plane from his uncle and would probably never be able to buy another. It was insured, but for nothing like replacement cost. That did remind him to snap a few pictures as they drew closer, including the identification or N-numbers near the tail.

They soon discovered the engine-compartment door had been damaged when the struts tore free and the plane skidded on its belly. Nate joined Alex in pulling on the handle, but in the end, they used a multitool to pry the door open and pull it up and back on its hinges. It kind of reminded him of opening a can of sardines.

Things were darker inside the compartment. Nate shone his light where Alex pointed. Tony Machi had told him exactly where the oil-tank plug was located and he levered himself down and around to be able to see if it was still there.

At first he thought it was missing. He snapped a few photos, sure something didn't look right, unsure what it was. He signaled to Nate to move the light to a different angle, and with different illumination, he finally figured out what he was looking at.

The plug was still screwed in place but there was a hole in it. It didn't make any sense. The engine oil would have easily leaked away within minutes through a hole that size and yet he'd been in the air long enough to get all the way to this lake before the situation became catastrophic.

He ran a finger across the opening, then moved aside so Nate could take a look. They took a few more pictures before kicking their way to the top of the plane. Alex studied the cracked and broken windshield for a moment, then peered through the open door he'd used to escape what could so easily have been his tomb.

He noticed his red leather-bound logbook on the Cessna's floor and signaled to Nate that he was going inside. The space was cramped and difficult to maneuver in with an aqua lung strapped to his back and a million of his own bubbles blocking his view. He was extremely careful not to get tangled up in the wreckage as he reached down and snagged the book.

Nate tapped him on the shoulder and Alex twisted around to find Nate pointing at the cabin floor. Alex looked. He didn't see anything noteworthy and attempted a shrug in an effort to ask Nate what he wanted.

Nate held his hand up to his mouth and made drinking gestures, then pointed at the floor again. All Alex could see down there were three or four unopened bottles of his favorite water. He twisted around to pick one of them up and held it toward Nate who took it from him and moved away from the opening so Alex could exit.

They swam away toward the surface without looking back. The FAA would pull the Cessna from the lake for their investigation, but Alex knew he might never see it again.

"JESS?"

Jessica opened her eyes, stunned that she'd actually fallen asleep. Alex was on his knees inside the shelter, right beside her. A wave of guilt washed through her as she looked into his eyes.

She started to sit up. "I'm so sorry—" she began, but stopped as she caught the look on his face as he scanned his humble sleeping space. "I should have waited for you," she finished.

He sat down next to her. He was dressed again, but his hair was still damp and he smelled like cold, fresh water.

"Where are Nate and Sarah?"

"Back on the shore. Sarah built a fire. I told them I wanted to come find you by myself."

She nodded as she blinked sleep away. When he spoke again, his voice sounded contemplative. "It all seems like a bizarre nightmare," he said as he looked around the small space.

"Did you find anything on the plane?"

He told her about the hole in the oil-tank plug. "I also found my logbook and took that. The FAA might quibble with me about it, but as far as I'm concerned it's part diary, as well, and I don't want a bunch of strangers reading it."

"I don't blame you," she said.

"Nate had me grab a bottle of my water, too," he added.

"Why?"

"He's convinced they were tampered with. I don't see how. I bought a six-pack of them the night before and stowed them on the plane myself. There was nothing about them to suggest they were anything but what they appeared to be. Still, we'll get it tested. I've learned to pay attention to Nate when he has a hunch."

They fell silent for a minute until Jessica leaned her head against his shoulder. "I like the way you decorated the place," she said, glancing up again at her own image, drawn in charcoal on a rock face.

They both lay down and looked up. She rested her head on his arm. "I can't tell you how many hundreds of dreams I had about you while I was sleeping right here on this bed," he said. He kissed her brow and squeezed her. "Some of them were pretty damn erotic."

"I bet they were."

"Yeah. And some were terrifying."

"How were they terrifying?"

"I'd dream you were in danger and I couldn't get to you. Once I dreamed you'd fallen through the ice into the freezing water below and I was grabbing for your hand, but you kept drifting further and further away and you never said a word or even struggled."

She pressed herself closer to him.

"But the worst one was when I walked into our house after miraculously getting home and it was empty. No furniture, no nothing, especially, no you."

"Oh, Alex," she said softly.

"Because you see, I thought for sure I'd blown it and that even if I was rescued or managed to get out of these mountains, you would have moved on with your life…you would have let me go."

"But I didn't," she said. She closed her eyes for a second before adding, "I want to tell you something."

"What? Are you all right? Is the baby okay?"

"Yes, I'm fine, it's nothing like that. It's about something I did while you were away."

He looked up at the drawing he'd made of her, then over into her eyes. "I know about the Facebook page."

She took a deep breath. "Oh."

"Dylan mentioned it."

"When?"

"Days ago."

"But you didn't say anything to me."

"There didn't seem any point."

"I could have tried to explain," she said.

He pulled her closer. "You don't have to explain," he said.

"Yes, I do," she mumbled. She took another deep breath. "You can't imagine what it was like to find out I was pregnant right on the eve of your disappearance. I'd dreamed about telling you that news a million times, but then you were gone, and I couldn't bear it. Not just because I loved you, but because this was something you wanted as much as I did and you might never know."

"I understand," he said.

"Do you? I'm not sure I do. It was crazy to think you'd run away from me, but it was also comforting because it meant you weren't dead. If you'd just gotten sick of me, then maybe you were living somewhere and maybe if you were alive, you would think of me sometimes and then perhaps you'd check out my Facebook page. So I wrote that if you could, you should call me. No questions asked, no problems, there was just something you needed to know. In a way it made a ringing phone easier to handle because it might actually be...you."

"I'm so sorry, Jess," he said, kissing her face.

She ran a hand over his cheek, smoothing his hair away from his brow. His eyes glowed as he looked down at her.

"In my head I believed you were dead," she whispered. "In my heart I wanted you alive, somewhere, anywhere. I told myself you didn't have to come back to me if you didn't love me, but you should know about your baby."

"Why didn't you tell me all this when I got home?"

"I was ashamed of myself."

He held her tighter. In a way she wished they could stay in that camp together, just the two of them. "Why were you so reluctant for me to see this place?" she asked after a little while.

"I'm not sure. I guess I just wanted to forget how miserable and unhappy I was most of the time. Having you see it made me feel like it would all seem too real."

"But it is real, Alex, and now that I've seen it and shared it with you, it's more real than ever. And it's remarkable you managed to survive with so little, that you got out alive, that we have a second chance to be together."

He wiped the tears off her cheek. "Until now," he whispered, "I wasn't sure we were together, I mean in a way that would last. But we are, aren't we?"

She nodded as he kissed her, as he ran his hands over her body. "So, where do we go from here?" he asked, his voice as soft as silk against her neck, warm like honey.

She put her hands on either side of his face and looked right into his eyes. "We go home. We find out who killed Billy and Lynda Summers—"

"If they were both murdered—"

"Of course they were both murdered. We find out who did it and we stop them from killing anyone else." She paused for a second as she ran a finger across his lips. "Especially you."

"Especially us," he amended, wrapping both arms around her and touching her lips with his.

His breath was warm and fresh, his kisses intoxicating. She reached up and tugged on his shirt. "How'd you like to make some new memories on this bed of yours?"

"What kind of memories?" he whispered.

"This kind," she said, and slowly started unbuttoning her blouse.

He took over the unbuttoning process. "Are you sure?" he asked. He followed this question with a dozen kisses along her throat.

"I'm sure," she said softly. Those were the last words uttered for quite some time.

Her clothes came off in a hurry, and then she helped him with his. There was something so natural about lying in this bed made of boughs with sunlight glinting through the woven branches, the quiet afternoon ethereal and complete. Only their breathing and the rustle of the dried leaves and twigs broke the silence as they touched each other in all the ways they'd learned over the years brought pleasure, pausing once to just stare at each other in a sense of amazement.

When they were both stripped, he fondled her breasts and kissed them, his mouth hot and intoxicating. She closed her eyes, only to open them when she felt both his hands on her abdomen. He leaned down and kissed her right beneath the belly button, then moved lower. Flames leaped inside her at the touch of his tongue and she frantically reached for him, delighting in the silky smoothness of his body, groaning in pleasure as his fingers ran over her contours.

He entered her when they both reached the point

of absolute no return, when to delay another second would be unimaginable. His thrusts were gentle in a way she'd never experienced from him before, as though he was afraid he would hurt her or their baby, and she quickly dispelled him of such thoughts by pushing down on his rear and raising her hips to meet him. She could tell the moment he was lost to reason and she willfully and gladly followed him, swept up in his responses and her own body's greedy need for him.

They lay still afterward, and then dressed each other slowly, with kisses and smiles, both realizing they stood at the cusp of a new beginning in their lives together.

It seemed to Jessica that all they had to do was survive the present and the future was theirs for the taking.

Chapter Ten

By the time they flew back to Blunt Falls and landed on John Miter's lake, the day was drifting away. John met them at the dock where Alex taxied.

John was a good-looking guy of sixty or so with a full head of silver hair and a permanent tan. With a knowing glint in his gray eyes, he helped Sarah and Jessica disembark. "You guys find what you were looking for?" he asked.

"And how do you know we were looking for something?" Jessica asked with a smile.

"I just have a feeling," he said. "Well?"

"I'm not sure. Alex, what in the world is this?"

As she spoke, she lifted the recovered bottle of Vita-Drink whose label had long ago disintegrated. It was still damp although it had been laying in a towel. When she hefted it, her fingers must have slid on the accumulated goo that had attached itself to the outside. The compression of her grasping it produced a tiny spurt of the purplish fluid to hit her on the arm.

"It's one of your drinks," she said, using the towel to wipe away months of slime.

"Is it open?" Alex asked.

She started to twist the cap. The pressure from her fingers released another tiny spout of fluid. "The cap is on tight," she said, "but it's got a leak." By now they were all standing close to each other staring at the Vita-Drink. "You think this was drugged?" she added. "But the cap is still sealed."

Nate took his key ring out of his pocket and separated a tiny flashlight from the keys. He shined it on the bottle. "Squeeze it again, Jess."

She did so and yet another squirt shot through the air and hit Alex in the middle of the chest. "There it is, see? A tiny hole, up high on the shoulder of the plastic bottle."

"Maybe it deteriorated under the water," Jessica said, though her voice hinted that even she didn't believe that.

"That's the kind of hole a hypodermic needle makes," Sarah said as she peered intently.

"You were drugged," Nate said, gripping Alex's arm.

Again Alex stared at the fluid. It looked so innocent.

"Who knew you drank these when you flew?" Sarah asked.

It was Jessica and Nate who laughed. "Everyone who knows him knows he's addicted to these things."

"I wouldn't exactly call it an addiction," Alex said, but he knew his fondness for them was common knowledge at work, at home, at the airport—everywhere.

Alex gently took the bottle and looked at the liquid through the clear plastic. "But I didn't notice a different smell or taste." He lifted his shirt and sniffed the spot the liquid had hit. He could detect no strange odor.

"We need to have it tested," Jessica said. "The police lab—"

"No," Alex and Nate said in tandem.

"I don't want to advertise I took anything off the plane," Alex explained.

"What about your logbook?" Jessica asked. The book was sealed inside a plastic bag.

"That's personal," he said. "I left all the flight information for the feds to find. I don't know if any of the log is readable anymore but like I told you, I don't want some government lab worker going through my daily entries. Nor am I going to admit I took the drink. We'll have to find an independent lab."

He'd been so quiet they'd all but forgotten that John Miter still stood nearby. He spoke up now. "I'll get it analyzed if you want."

Alex looked him in the eye. He might not know

a lot about Miter's past—or frankly, anything at all—but he did have a good gut feeling about the guy. "You know of one?"

Miter smiled. "Yes."

"How?"

Miter laughed softly. "Leave it to me," he said.

Nate caught Alex's gaze and Alex could see he was unsure. After all, Nate didn't know John. "I want a sample of it to take back to Arizona," Nate said. "It's better if we split it up."

"I agree," Alex said.

Jessica found a couple of small bottles of seltzer in the ice chest in which they'd packed their lunch, and poured out the contents. Alex transferred a third of the old vitamin drink to one empty bottle, a third to another, and handed them to John and Nate respectively.

"You don't quite trust me," John said, his eyes glinting.

"I don't quite trust anyone," Alex said, "though I deeply appreciate all the help you've been."

Miter's gaze was direct and intense and, truthfully, intimidating, and then he smiled and took the sample. "Smart man," he said, and laughing, checked the twist top.

AFTER THEY DROVE Nate and Sarah to the airport, Alex and Jessica continued on to the Machi house. It had been a long, emotionally draining day for both of them, full of highs and lows and discoveries. And yet Alex felt connected to his life in a way he hadn't in longer than he cared to remember.

He wasn't as certain as Jessica that Lynda Summers's death hadn't been an accident. It didn't seem to him the woman knew much about her son's life even though he lived in her house. What threat could Lynda have posed for anyone unless she was into something herself that Alex knew nothing about? Why would someone murder her?

Had she seen or heard someone that night Billy went missing?

The coroner had said Billy was unconscious when he met his death. There was no proof Billy had ridden his bike to the drive-in. Tomorrow, Alex planned to drive the road between Billy's house and his own, looking for someone who might have seen Billy late that night. Maybe he'd met his attacker along that road. Or maybe he'd made it all the way home and gone out back to the shed without checking in with his mother who it appeared slept in front of the television every night. Maybe Lynda had heard her son's abductor.

"I've been wanting to ask you what the chief said when you called him this morning and told him you weren't coming in today," Jessica said as they pulled up outside a modest house in a forty-year-old subdivision. A few toys lay scattered across the front lawn while a couple of cars and a truck were parked in the driveway.

"I told him I wasn't feeling well. I admit I didn't like lying to him. Frank Smyth isn't as bad as I thought he was. I just had to do this today."

She smiled at him. "You don't sound much like the job-first-at-any-cost cop I married, you know."

"Maybe I've finally grown up. There is nothing more important to me than you and our baby."

"I know," she said softly.

"But it's even more than that," he admitted. "Seeing my plane, listening to Nate, well, you know, the big hits the country has taken from foreign terrorists are terrible and frightening. But somehow, we rally afterward, we declare a common enemy, we convince ourselves, over time, that we can prepare ourselves, protect ourselves." He stared straight ahead, then glanced at her.

"This is different. These people aim lower and closer to the belly, if you know what I mean. Their goal isn't massive loss of life, it's loss of well-being, of the safety of doing mundane things or observing traditional events. It's Americans going after other Americans. It's power hungry people manipulating innocents into thinking with their adrenaline instead of their heads, listening to their fears instead of their consciences. They have to be stopped."

"I know," she said softly. They were silent for

a moment before she added, "Your friend John Miter is a little spooky."

"I know."

"I'm glad you didn't give him all that Vita-Drink. If I had to choose someone who might be in on a plot of some kind, I guess he would come to mind."

"He does look the part, I grant you that. But remember, I met him way before Labor Day last year and the fact that Nate and Mike and I got involved in that mall shooting and subsequently everything else was pure chance. Nate and I went to a mall because of a delayed flight with nothing on our minds other than finding something to eat in the food court. Mike told us he was there because he needed new jeans and they were having a sale at one of the stores. It was just chance."

"I'm still glad Nate took some of the water with him."

"And we have the bottle. Okay, let's go talk to Tony."

Tony's wife, Noreen, insisted they sit at the table and have a piece of strawberry pie, an offer neither Alex nor Jessica felt inclined to refuse. She was as friendly and generous as her husband, balancing kids and home like a seasoned pro.

Alex took out his camera, and while they ate pie, downloaded his pictures onto Tony's computer. While Jessica helped Noreen clear away the dishes, Alex and Tony studied the photographs.

"These are pretty clear," Tony said, scanning the images.

Alex used the tip of a pencil to point at the screen. "This is the cap," he said.

"Holy hell!" Tony murmured, leaning closer to study the image. "The safety twist wire is completely gone. And what's that hole? Do you have a better picture?"

Alex scrolled until they found one taken from a different perspective.

"Yeah," Tony said, touching the screen. "That's the hole right there. Straight through the plug. Damn, I wish you could have brought it to me."

"I do, too."

Tony sat back in his chair. "Someone drilled the center out of the plug and replaced it with something else," he said.

"I know. What I don't understand is why it lasted so long before it blew. If it was secure enough to get the plane in the air why did it suddenly give way?"

"Maybe it was some kind of wax," Tony said.

"Wouldn't it just melt when the engine got hot?"

"Yeah, but it might take a while. Once it melted away, though, that would be it. The oil would leak out, the engine would seize—"

"Which is exactly what happened."

"And they might have mixed in some other product that would delay the melting of the wax. There may be residue on the plug. If there is, the FAA will find it."

"But, Tony, how did the plug get there? You did the maintenance yourself and it's not exactly an easy spot for someone to tamper with out on the field."

Tony ran a hand through his thinning hair and shook his head. "The FAA looked through all my stuff, checked inventory lists, the whole nine yards. There wasn't anything missing that should have been there and that includes those plugs. I'd just received a shipment of five in that size, you know the Airtop brand in the red-and-yellow box. I'd used two of them, one on your plane and one on Vic Miller's. The other three were all where they were supposed to be, just like everything else. I'll have to review my records to see where they were all installed and make sure they weren't tampered with, too."

Alex stood behind Tony, who sat in front of the computer, and stared at the images on the screen. He was still staring at them a moment later when Jessica slipped her hand into his.

"Could Billy have switched plugs while you were eating lunch?" Alex finally asked. He felt Jessica's grip tighten around his fingers.

Tony swiveled in his chair and looked up at him. "What do you mean?"

"Think about it for a moment. Could Billy have taken out the plug you put in after the oil change and replaced it with this one?"

Tony turned back around to the screen, studied the photographs, then turned back. "If you mean could he have physically switched out the plugs, I guess, sure, maybe. Let me think. I did that part of the checkup, took a break, came back and finished the maintenance."

"Does that include refilling the oil tank?"

"It would have to. If anyone had tried to switch the plug after the oil was already installed, there would have been a big puddle on the floor."

"I can't imagine Billy could do all that," Jessica said softly.

Tony looked back at her. "It's not really that hard. He would have had to snip the safety twist wire is all, then take out the good plug and put in the drilled out one."

"So someone would have had to give him the doctored plug and pretty clear instructions?" Jessica said.

"Yes."

"And instructed him exactly how to exchange it?"

"Yes. All they'd have to do is Google it." He

swore under his breath. "He was acting odd that day. I should have known something was wrong."

"And just so we're clear," Alex continued, "if this is the way it happened, it's possible you wouldn't have noticed the switch when you came back after lunch, is that right?"

Tony was quiet for a second, and then he shook his head. "No, I wouldn't have noticed. I imagine the plugs looked exactly alike unless you were really looking for a difference and I was already finished with that part of the job."

"But how would someone have known exactly what plug your engine took?" Jessica asked.

Tony answered the question. "Most of the Cessna 180s like Alex's came with Continental engines. That would mean drains and equipment would differ from one year to the next. But if someone knew what year Alex's plane was built, the rest wouldn't be hard to figure and with the N-number on the tail, checking it out would be pretty easy."

So it could have been almost anyone, Alex thought as Jessica leaned her head against his shoulder.

Tony once again ran his hand through his hair. "I can't believe Billy would do this. He knew whose plane we were working on." He looked back up at Alex. "What in the world did the boy have against you?"

"I don't know," Alex said, then added, "Probably nothing."

Tony shook his head again.

Blue Point Road didn't have a whole lot of residences within view of the highway. Places out here tended to sit back from the road a bit, some with heavily wooded areas between the houses and traffic. And one side of the pavement was nothing but a steep fall into a gorge.

Working their way toward the Summers house, Alex and Dylan drove down five driveways. No one was home at two of them, one man had absolutely nothing to offer and the elderly couple at the fifth went to bed every night by nine o'clock, rain or shine.

The last house looked as though it would present another no-one-is-home moment. The road was densely covered with arching trees and Dylan swore under his breath as some of the limbs hit his car. "I just got it back from the shop," he complained. "Cripes, doesn't anyone around here prune stuff?"

This was the first time Alex had seen Dylan's new car and it was a beauty. Built low to the ground, power seemed to ooze from under the hood. In many ways, the car was a perfect fit for the well-toned man who drove it.

"How did you get the car back from Billings?" Alex asked.

"I figured you can get a pizza delivered, you can get a car delivered," he said.

They finally reached the house and knocked at the front door. No response until a woman's voice called from the back. The two of them walked around the well-kept cabin to emerge in a beautifully tended garden that boasted lush vegetable beds as well as walls of climbing flowers. As the growing season started late and ended early in parts of Montana, there wasn't actually a lot of produce on the plants yet but even to Alex's untrained eye, the vegetation looked lavish and healthy.

The owner of the voice rose from where she'd been sitting on the side of a raised flower bed. It had turned into a warm day and she wore a skimpy T-shirt with a flowing cotton skirt and sandals. She'd piled her blondish hair atop her head where it tumbled over her eyes. Her voice was whiskey soaked and her expression was saucy. She was probably in her late forties and holding her own.

"Can I help you?" she asked, the spade in front of her.

"Excuse us," Alex said with a swift glance at Dylan who was giving the woman his customary once-over that seemed to take a week. After introducing themselves, he explained, "We're investigating the death of a man who lived up the street, Billy Summers. We're hoping you might have seen or heard something late Saturday night, early Sunday morning."

"Heard something?" she asked, settling her hip against a potting bench. "Like what?"

"Like a car passing or screech of metal or maybe you saw Billy on his bike?"

"Oh," she said. "No, I didn't. I wish I could help. I know who Billy was. Sometimes he stopped by to see my garden. Not this year, not yet, anyway, and now I hear he's dead, that someone ran over him. That's too bad, he was a sweet guy."

"Thanks for your time," Dylan said as he handed her a card. "If you think of anything, please give us a call."

Her assurances followed them back to the front yard.

"She was holding up pretty good for an old broad," Dylan commented.

"Damn, man, keep your voice down." Alex lightened his tone and added, "What in the world would a real woman see in a clown like you, anyway?"

"Sticks and stones," Dylan crooned.

Once they hit the road, Alex pointed toward the Summers house. "Go that way," he said. "Lynda Summers had closer neighbors we can interview."

"We already talked to them," Dylan said.

"They were questioned about *her* death. I want to ask them if they heard anything the night Billy disappeared. But, frankly, I want another look around the Summers place, too."

"You're becoming obsessed," Dylan said, but then he shook his head. "Sorry. After what you told me you found on the Cessna, of course you're obsessed." He poked Alex in the ribs. "I knew you weren't sitting home sick because I drove by your place and no one was there."

"Why did you do that?"

Dylan shrugged. "I just doubted you were sick and thought you might need help of some kind. Why didn't you tell me you were going to dive on the plane? You told that Miter guy."

"I just borrowed a plane from John," Alex said. "If he knows anything else it's because he always seems to know exactly what's going on."

"I know. That's what creeps me out about him."

"Anyway, it all came up kind of fast."

"I can read between the lines," Dylan said. "You didn't want the chief to blab it to his reporter pal."

"Something like that," Alex said.

"I still can't believe Billy had anything to do with your crash," Dylan said. "Frankly, the kid didn't seem clever enough."

"If he did, he must have had help," Alex said.

"Yeah. Maybe Tad and Ted Cummings put him up to it."

Alex was about to protest but stopped himself. How did he know what Tad and Ted were capable of?

"Maybe Billy's death didn't have much to do with drugs," Dylan mused aloud. "If the Cummings boys were in on the conspiracy to keep you from going to Shatterhorn, maybe they decided to cut their weakest link—Billy—out of the picture."

Alex glanced over. "What?"

Dylan shifted position which seemed to cause the car to sway. Sitting next to the guy in the low-slung car was like sitting next to a bulging muscle. "Think about it," he said. "Didn't that B-Strong organization in Shatterhorn use young males about Ted and Tad's age to do their dirty work?"

"They trained them as gunmen who then terrorized malls and picnics and parades," Alex said. "We'd better check them out for any kind of club involvement."

"Is there a B-Strong around here?"

"From what Nate said, there's no longer any B-Strong clubs anywhere. They were disbanded after what they were doing came to light."

Dylan parked in the yard. The old double-wide already had a sagging look of abandonment about it, like the weight of its interior was pulling the roof down and in. There was a sign on the door telling people the property was condemned and to keep out.

"Things move fast," Alex said.

"They sure do," Dylan said as he rubbed a tiny scratch on his hood with a finger and swore under his breath. "Okay. I'll take the two houses down there, you get the three up the street."

They went their separate ways. The first house Alex came to was owned by a small, ancient-looking woman. She tried to think back to Saturday night or early Sunday morning, but Alex could see it was a lost cause.

"I don't go outside after dark," she finished. "There's that woman next door and her odd son. Have you seen what a mess she keeps that place? It's disgraceful. I have half a mind to call the mayor."

There was no one home at the house next to hers, and at the house farthest away, he found several people sitting around the yard drinking beer. Figuring out which person actually owned the place took a while and produced no results. Alex walked back to the Summers place. Unless Dylan had better luck, this line of inquiry was going nowhere fast.

He waited in the yard for Dylan to return for five long minutes and in that time, he had the strangest feeling that someone was watching him. He walked completely around the house and saw nothing, didn't even hear anything but some birds chattering up in the treetops.

Eventually, he decided to take another look at the shed while he waited. It was once again locked, and Alex played around with breaking it open to look at the model airplanes and the room one more time. Instead he walked around to the back where he saw evidence the lab crew had tried to lift footprints from under the window. Stepping carefully to avoid the last of the yellow crime-scene tape, he moved the ivy and peered into the room.

His gaze was immediately drawn to the stack of index cards beside the lamp. He was almost positive there had been more there the first time he saw it, though he couldn't say why that thought persisted. He closed his eyes and tried to picture it the way it had looked the first time he'd seen the room. The striped lamp, the cards by the base, all the way up to the bottom of the first yellow line.

He opened his eyes. That was it. The cards topped out down low on a black stripe. The stack was shorter than it had been before Billy died.

"What are you doing?" Dylan asked.

Caught by surprise, Alex jumped a few inches. Then he told Dylan about the index cards.

"Are you sure?" Dylan asked.

"Well, I guess I wouldn't bet my life on it, but I'm pretty sure."

"Maybe Lynda took some of them when she came to unlock the shed," Dylan offered.

"And that doesn't make sense, either. If she was so grief-stricken she was on sedatives, why would she have walked out here by herself to unlock the shed and then come inside to investigate? Why would she do that?"

"From everything you and Frank Smyth have said, I get the impression she wasn't aware of what Billy had done to the inside of the place. Maybe it caught her off guard. Where did we come up with the scenario that she came outside to unlock it?"

Alex thought for a second. "Chief Smyth surmised it. We don't know for sure." What caused him to pause was the fact that he'd found Smyth inside the shed when he came looking for him the day Lynda died. Was it possible he'd slipped some of the index cards into a pocket? He'd actually been standing next to the lamp and table.

But why do it with everyone there when he'd apparently enjoyed free access to this place? And wouldn't taking those cards amount to a cover-up, either for himself or someone else? Was Alex really thinking that the chief of their small police department was involved in all this?

He tried to recall the man's politics as he moved aside for Dylan who had been straining to see into the room over Alex's shoulder. But he didn't know Frank that well. He'd never been to his house or said more than a greeting to his wife or met his daughter. Still, could a man be part of something so sinister and not reveal it in his everyday life?

If he was clever enough.

This was impossible.

Again Alex thought back to the day before yesterday. He'd commented on the scratches on the back of Frank's hand. He could visualize the chief subsequently shoving that hand in a pocket. He'd been wearing the kind of jacket someone wears when they ride a bike, close fitting, not bulky at all. Wouldn't Alex have seen the general shape of a half a dozen or more cards if they'd been in one of those pockets?

Dylan walked away from the window and Alex took his place for one last glimpse. This time he noticed a small vertical seam on the rounded side of the table. He'd taken it for a defect, but now he wondered if it indicated an inset drawer. Why hadn't he paid more attention to it when he had the chance?

"All we have are questions and more questions," he muttered to himself. He glanced at Dylan. "You were gone quite a while. Did you find out anything?"

"Nobody was home anywhere," Dylan said. "I swear, this neck of the woods empties out during the day. I'll catch them tomorrow night." He popped a knuckle or two.

"Why not tonight?"

"I have plans."

"Are you driving all the way back to Billings to see your new girlfriend?"

"How'd you guess?"

"And you have the nerve to call me obsessed."

"Get in and relax," Dylan said with a laugh.

Alex slid into the luxurious car, but the relaxing part wasn't as easy to accomplish. On the way back into town, he found himself checking his side mirror, trying to see if they were being followed.

He never saw a thing but he was almost certain someone was there.

Chapter Eleven

Jessica was as restless that night as Alex was. Neither of them could stand staying inside the house. Since their own yard still held too many upsetting memories they tried a walk. Even that didn't settle their nerves.

They finally decided to drive to the store and order the flowers for Memorial Day. That process ate up a whole forty-five minutes. They were waiting in a long line to buy a sandwich for dinner when Alex's cell phone rang.

"It's John Miter," Alex said as he scanned the screen.

What followed was a short conversation where Alex hardly said anything but listened intently until he muttered, "No rush, we're not at home. Thanks."

"Was that about the Vita-Drink?" Jessica asked as he pocketed his phone. She'd unconsciously lowered her voice as though the people in line behind them had the slightest idea what they were talking about. It was just sometimes hard to remember that not everyone was caught up in the same confusing drama they were.

"John's friends at the lab just got back to him. Nate is right, the drink was drugged." His voice was toned way down, too. "He'll email the results to our home computer sometime tonight."

"What drugs?"

"A whole laundry list of pharmaceuticals. Something to relax muscles, something else to make you sleepy—it was probably the combination of them that made me queasy as well as tired that morning. It's a wonder I didn't pass out."

"Who could have done this?" she asked.

"I picked up the water at the store the night before the flight. It was locked in my truck in our garage until I got to the airport the next morning. Someone either doctored the bottles there or switched them with previously altered bottles that morning, and the only time I can think either of those things could have been done was when Kit called me at the airport and I went inside to take his call."

"Why didn't he call on your cell?"

"He said he was at home and he didn't have that number. Let's see, I remember him complaining that he hadn't been able to reach Dylan. Anyway, it was a miserable morning weatherwise, cold and nasty and the only other person I saw on the field was Billy Summers."

"But you said he was cleaning a windshield or something like that."

"Deicing, I think, but I didn't see him working, I just saw him carrying a bunch of stuff."

"Coming or going?"

"He was coming toward me while I was walking to the Cessna."

"So you think he could have been carrying your original water bottles?" she whispered.

"They could have been in the toolbox," he agreed as he dug out his keys. "Let's get out of here."

"Where are we going?"

"Blue Point Road. You game?"

"Absolutely," she said.

ALEX STOPPED AT the first of the three houses Dylan had struck out with that afternoon and was relieved when someone was home. Jessica sat in the car as he conducted the brief interview, which didn't turn out to help a whole lot because the guy admitted he fell asleep to a blaring television every night.

The second place appeared to be abandoned but the man who answered Alex's knock at the last house was a different story. He claimed he'd heard screeching brakes late Saturday night.

"What time?" Alex asked.

The guy was in his late forties, tall, wearing a bib apron printed with the slogan Will Cook for Sex. He explained he had to flip a steak on his indoor grill in exactly four minutes. The aroma of sizzling beef wafting from the kitchen started Alex's stomach rumbling.

"After midnight. The clock in the bedroom is broken but I'd gone to bed at twelve and I heard the brakes before I actually fell asleep."

"Did you see anything?"

"I looked out the window. I think I saw a couple of lights like headlamps a little bit south of here, but it was really foggy and I'm not sure. That road is treacherous on a bad night." He glanced at his wristwatch. "It's time to turn the T-bone. You need anything else?"

Alex handed him a card. He got back in the truck, and together he and Jessica drove south, stopping often to look at the road. About four hundred feet along, Alex found what he was looking for and got out to check the pavement.

When he got back inside after taking a half dozen pictures with his cell phone, Jessica raised her eyebrows. "Well?"

"There are tire tracks like a vehicle makes with a sudden stop, but there's no way for me to know when they were made or by who. I'll call downtown and get someone out here tomorrow to process them just to be on the safe side." He was thinking the adjacent terrain deserved a once-over, as well.

It was still light outside, though the shadows were deepening when they pulled up in front of Billy's old house. Alex was surprised to find a tractor and a large Dumpster out front.

"What's with the equipment?" Jessica asked as Alex parked his truck.

"I don't know," he said. "I wonder who will end up with this place."

"What would anyone do with it?"

"I can't imagine. Probably knock it down once it clears probate. The land must be worth something. Come on, let's make sure no one else is around, and then take another look at that shed, okay?"

They both got out of the truck and Alex took Jessica's hand. He wasn't sure exactly how they'd managed to go from lovers and friends to frustrated near enemies, and he also wasn't sure how they had managed to get back on the right track with each other. Perhaps they owed this second chance to the plane crash which was kind of ironic when you thought about it.

But wonderful, too. It was hard to believe that they would soon be parents at long last.

"Which room are we going to turn into a nursery?" he asked suddenly.

She looked up at him and smiled and he leaned

over to kiss the top of her head as his arm slipped around her shoulders. "I thought the one right across the hall from ours," she said after a moment.

"Do we know if it's a girl or boy yet?"

"Not yet. The ultrasound that checks bone length and organ development also reveals the baby's sex. It's in about a week."

"Which do you want?" he asked, stopping to pat her stomach area and look into her eyes.

"I couldn't care less," she said. "How about you?"

"One of each," he said lightly as he stepped onto the front porch and knocked, then tried the knob. "It's locked," he announced. He looked through the window, too. The place looked different than it had when he'd last been there which was right after Lynda Summers's death, as if more of the boxes had been shifted here and there. No doubt the paramedics had had to rearrange things to get Lynda's body out of her house.

"Let's go around back," he said.

He called out as they walked around the house, not wanting to surprise anyone, but there wasn't anybody there.

The shed door was secured just as it had been earlier that afternoon, with a lock threaded through a hasp. "Wait here a second," he said, and sprinted back to his truck where he took a toolbox out of the covered bed and carried it back to the shed. Setting it on the ground, he dug around in it until he found a screwdriver.

"Alex Foster, what are you doing?" Jessica asked, her eyes wide.

"I'm taking the hasp off the door because I don't want to break the lock."

"Is that legal?"

"Not technically."

"In what way, then?"

He removed the last screw from the old wood and the hasp came free. "I think Billy tried to kill me."

"I know you do."

"And I think he must have had help and I don't know who that person might be. That makes trusting anyone except you a little tricky. Plus there's a tractor and a rig out front. On the off chance I missed something in this shed, I plan on taking a look before it's too late. Stay here."

"Who's going to watch your back?" she said. "If we're caught, maybe we can share a cell."

Alex laughed as he stepped inside the shed, Jessica right behind him. The laughter died immediately. Billy's bastion of uncluttered order looked as though it had been hit by a tornado. Glass sparkled on the floor in front of the shattered window and the little striped lamp had been smashed to pieces. The round table lay on its side next to the overstuffed chair that spilled its foam rubber guts.

"Someone has been in here," Alex said unnecessarily. As he righted the table, he noticed something was missing and looked around the room.

"This was Billy's space?" Jessica said.

"I know it's hard to believe, but it used to look like a little oasis next to everything else around here," Alex said.

"Why would anyone destroy it this way?"

"It looks to me like someone was looking for something."

"I wonder if they found it."

"If it was part of the red-and-white biplane that used to hang over the table, it appears so. The plane is gone and I don't see its pieces on the floor."

"There are other models."

"This one was different. Much larger, better constructed."

She stared at the ones that had survived the attack. "He was capable of being very creative," she said.

"Yeah."

"When I think of how meticulous he was with the garden—you know, Alex, I'm going to replant it. I can't let whoever did that to Billy's work get away with it, especially when they also wrecked this sanctuary. I mean it has to be the work of the same person, don't you think?"

"It sure appears to have the same wanton destruction-for-destruction's-sake quality about it," he agreed.

"Yeah. Well, I'm going to make our yard beautiful again, you know, in his memory."

"That's a good idea," Alex said. He looked down at the table and used his fingers to feel for the groove in the table apron that he'd noticed from the window. "I was right, it's a drawer," he said, kneeling in order to check it out and watching he didn't cut himself on broken glass. He turned the table a little and slid out the drawer that seemed to have a spring mechanism instead of a knob or handle. "This seems shallow," he said.

"Is there anything in it?"

"Not much. I don't want to leave prints on the contents, though. I should have brought gloves."

"Wait a second," she said. "I just saw an open box of latex gloves over in the mess on Billy's workbench."

"Don't touch anything," he cautioned. "I'll get them. I was here two days ago so my prints are easy to explain away but yours might be a different matter."

"That's why my hands are in my pockets," she said. "I'm married to a cop, you know. I figure stuff like this out."

He grabbed a couple of gloves so he wouldn't destroy any evidence that might be in the drawer, and stopped to kiss her forehead before he once again knelt in front of the drawer.

"Okay. There are a few blank index cards, a couple of pencils…not much else. Frankly there doesn't seem to be room for much else."

She knelt beside him, touching her belly as she did so. "For the first time, it feels like there's a baby between my chest and my knees when I bend over," she said, and they exchanged excited smiles. She studied the drawer before adding, "Is that a false bottom?"

"Yeah, I think it is," he said as he withdrew his knife. Wishing the light were better, he inserted the blade at the front edge of the drawer bottom and immediately felt the thin wood wobble. He removed the few things that had been scattered atop the false bottom, then carefully slipped the wood out of place.

They found themselves staring at a hypodermic needle and three small empty medical vials whose labels Alex recognized as the drugs John Miters's lab had confirmed were injected into the Vita-Drink bottles.

Beside him, Jessica's sigh sounded like a very soft, sad refrain. "I didn't want to believe it," she said.

"Look," he said as he lifted the needle out of the

drawer to reveal an index card covered with simple illustrations and directions. "Here's how you load a needle with the drugs and then inject the contents into the high shoulder of a plastic bottle. Sound familiar?"

"Of course it does."

He slid the entire drawer from the table and gestured at the index cards. "Is that Billy's writing?"

"I don't think so. What are we going to do with all this?"

After shifting the drawer into position under his arm, he helped Jessica stand. "I'm going to call downtown and get a crew out here," he said, grabbing his phone from his pocket. "I'll stay with everything until someone arrives. The place has already been broken into once tonight, we can't walk away and leave it unguarded."

"Actually," she said with a fleeting smile, "it was broken into twice."

"You and your technicalities," he said.

"What do you want me to do?"

"I want you to drive to Silvia's house. I want you as far away from all this as you can get." He pulled out his phone but before he could place a call, her fingers lit on his arm. He looked down at her.

"I'm not leaving you here alone," she said. "You should know that about me by now."

He did know it. He just wanted her to be safe and that meant away from this shed.

"Just make the call," she told him.

He nodded, but before he could tap even one number the window beside them shattered. From the corner of his eye, he saw a missile fly into the room. It hit the chair and immediately burst into flames. "Get out of here!" Alex yelled, pulling on Jessica's hand. The fire quickly spread to the wooden floor and then to the worktable where it ignited the solvents and paints stored on the shelf.

They reached the safety of the outside right before a small explosion inside the building signaled the beginning of the end. They ran to get as far away as they could.

Alex handed Jessica the drawer and pulled out his gun. She stood with her back against the house, her face pale in the weakening light. She clutched the drawer in one hand while she took her cell phone from her sweater pocket with the other.

"Are you all right?" he asked her.

"I'll live. I'll call the fire department."

"Stay here," he added, and took off to the front where he could hear what sounded like a far-off motor. Their attacker was getting away. By the time Alex rounded the corner, the yard was clear and nothing looked one bit different than it had since they entered the shed. The tractor still stood off to the side, the Dumpster beside it, Alex's truck pulled in close to one of the wrecks that occupied the side yard.

His head pounded with the images of what could have happened inside that shed, not to himself, but to Jessica and their baby. He'd thought earlier about irony, and how saving his marriage might have actually hinged on being stranded in the mountains for three months.

But now it occurred to him that coming home might have put a whole host of people in jeopardy. Billy and Lynda were dead, the Cummings twins were under investigation, his wife had been scared out of her wits half a dozen times.

He returned to Jessica, unsure what to do to protect her except to disappear again…and that was not an option. She'd set the drawer aside and found a garden hose and had turned it on. He took it from her and aimed the water higher into the flames.

"Did you see anything?" she asked.

"No," he said. The water pressure wasn't great and seemed to be having no positive effect, so he switched his efforts to making sure the blaze didn't spread to the house, the trees or any of the abandoned cars that stood nearby. It was a relief to hear screeching sirens. Within minutes, firemen had taken over, the bomb squad was waiting nearby and police cars started arriving.

Alex explained that what he'd seen was a Molotov cocktail, a gas bomb made out of a beer bottle, gasoline with a burning rag as a wick. He didn't add what everyone there knew—such things were easy to construct out of universally available materials. Anyone could have done it.

Kit Anderson acted fidgety and ill at ease as he ran around doing his best to take charge. As soon as he could, Alex steered Jessica toward his truck. The smell of a fire and the resulting ash was never a pleasant one, but with all the burning garbage in the lean-to, this one was particularly noxious and he didn't want her exposed to it.

Kit caught up with him. "Where are you going with that?" he asked, gesturing at the drawer and its contents tucked under one of Alex's arms.

"Downtown," Alex said succinctly.

Kit held out his hands. "I'll take it."

"No, thanks," Alex said, and continued walking. Kit trotted behind him.

"The chief said I should handle this kind of thing," he insisted.

Alex turned and looked over his shoulder. "The chief doesn't even know this stuff exists."

"Well, not what you're holding in particular," he said, "just evidence in general."

"Let me get this straight," Alex said. "The chief told you not to allow me to transport evidence?"

Kit looked uncomfortable as he shuffled a bit. "Yeah."

"Too bad," Alex said and kept walking, relieved when Kit fell behind.

He paid close attention to the road and was

relieved when he saw the landmark he'd chosen, the broken branch on an old oak tree, and subsequently the tire marks on the roadbed. They would be easy to find again in the daylight. He searched his mind for the feeling that someone was watching him, but it didn't come like it had earlier in the day. At least there was that.

A few minutes later, Jessica touched his arm. "You're pretty quiet," she said. "What are you thinking about?"

He glanced over at her beautiful face illuminated by the dashboard lights. "Why would the chief tell Kit to make sure I wasn't handling evidence?"

"Maybe Kit was lying. Maybe he just wants to control everything."

Alex thought for a moment longer. "No, I don't think Kit was lying. The guy doesn't exactly have a poker face." He thought for a few seconds longer and added, "You know, the first part of the equation is relatively simple."

"What equation?"

"The beginning, back when someone wanted me and Nate and Mike dead. We represented an immediate threat to the Shatterhorn Killer. I think he overreacted. He got someone to try to run Nate off the road when he was on his way to Nevada to meet with me and Mike. They got someone else to sabotage my airplane. And then they drove up to Mike's house and shot him dead.

"If things had gone according to their plans, Nate would have died in the desert north of Vegas in a car accident. I would have slammed into a handy mountain somewhere or imploded in the middle of a desert and there wouldn't have been a lot left of my plane. Forensics being what they are now, the government may have uncovered a conspiracy but it would have been a lot harder and if everything else hadn't happened the way it had, they might not have even looked for one."

"But Nate didn't die," Jessica said, her hand warm on his thigh, her voice very soft.

"No. And no one else has tried to hurt him since then. It appears he isn't a threat anymore."

"Someone is sure trying to get you," she said.

"Yeah, but by the oddest backdoor methods. Ruining our garden, killing the guileless kid they set up to sabotage my plane, perhaps killing his mother because, well, I don't know why. Add that fake call to the emergency room and frightening you—it's crazy."

"And it's escalating," Jessica said. "There was nothing tentative about lobbing a bomb into an occupied building."

"But if they just wanted me dead, why not kill me? Shoot me, stab me, you know. Why all these antics? Get it over with already."

"Be careful what you say," she told him. "The universe may be listening."

THEY AWOKE YET again to a ringing phone, only this time it was Agent Struthers. "I'm in kind of a hurry but I wanted you and your wife to know we just got word that the man known as William Tucker is actually named Charles Bond. He was thought to be dead, one of several victims in a very messy terrorist attack in New Orleans several years ago. He obviously survived the terrorist attack and used the opportunity to disappear. There's nothing to tie him to that attack and in fact, the people behind it were caught, tried and convicted. But Bond apparently took on a false identity and moved in with his ex-brother-in-law, aka the Shatterhorn Killer. It now appears Bond is the one who's been pulling the strings."

Alex rubbed the sleep from his eyes and muttered, "Do you know where he is now?"

"Unfortunately, no. His last call was yesterday and he mentioned leaving Seattle. He didn't give a clue to his destination."

"Okay," Alex said with a sigh. "Is Seattle still on alert?"

"Absolutely. He's proven he doesn't have to be around to cause mayhem. He's pretty good at coaxing other people to do it for him. There's another lead suggesting the target for a Memorial

Day attack in Seattle is a big food-and-wine festival. Security is being tightened."

"I hope they get the bastards," Alex said.

"So do we all. But it makes sense that after Nate foiled the parade attack a year ago, Bond might be hot to try the same thing on a different one. Use caution, Detective Foster. Stay alert."

"I will," Alex assured him. After turning off the phone, he met Jessica's nervous gaze and put his arms around her, nuzzling her neck. "You're the best thing that ever happened to me," he said softly.

"Oh, Alex. Was that about William Tucker or whatever his name is?"

He put his hands on her shoulders and held her a short distance away so he could look into her eyes. "His name is Charles Bond." He told her what Struthers had said.

"Then he could be on his way here?"

"Here, there or anywhere. Who knows?"

Tears spilled onto her cheeks and she buried her face against his chest.

He kissed her hair and raised her chin so he could look in her eyes. "I'm here for you, sweetheart."

She nodded. "I just want it to be over. And I thought if he was behind our yard and the emergency-room stunt and then the bomb last night, well, at least we'd know who our enemy was. But if he's been in Seattle..."

Her voice trailed off and he finished the sentence in his head, *then it could be anyone.*

She put her lips against his. "I love you so much, Alex."

He kissed her again, losing himself in her tender warmth. And then the nature of the kisses changed as they often did, grew deeper, longer, merging into one long cacophony of sensation that awakened every part of his body. "It's still pretty early," he whispered with a rasping voice while cupping one of her succulent breasts in his hand, dipping his head to lick her nipple through the silk of her gown.

"Let's make the most of it," she said, and pulled him down on top of her.

SOON AFTER, ALEX joined the team investigating the tire marks he'd found on Blue Point Road south of the Summers house the night before. Dylan showed up a few minutes later and walked beside Alex.

Alex's attention was divided between searching the ground for some other sign of mishap and the sight of Frank Smyth's car pulling off to the side of the road beside the police van. A spray of gravel suggested the chief was either in a hurry or distracted. He jumped out of his car and began talking to the techs.

"I heard about what happened to you and Jess last night," Dylan said at last. "I was too far away to respond."

"I know you were," Alex said, watching the chief. "Smyth didn't show up, either. We left so Kit could play detective all by himself."

"Well, I want you to know something," Dylan added.

"What?"

"I've been thinking about everything that's happened to you and Jessica. I took it all too lightly. Hell, man, you guys could have been killed last night. From now on, I have your back. I'm going to get to the bottom of whatever is going on or die trying."

Alex looked closely at his partner. He wasn't used to the serious tone he heard in Dylan's voice and it touched him. "Thanks," he said.

"Sure thing. And I mean it. However, you do realize the tire tracks on the roadbed could have been made days ago, like even when you were still up in the mountains."

"I know. I can't believe I've been home a week."

"Neither can I. And I want you to know that I would have gone back to those houses tonight like I said I would. You didn't have to do it for me."

"I know. I was just restless and needed something to do. You know, one of those places is totally empty."

"Guess that explains why no one answered the door."

The chief came to a stop near them, pausing for a second to shield a cigarette with his hand while he lit it with his trusty lighter. "I heard you were out here," he said, addressing Alex. "I also heard what happened last night. Is your wife okay?"

"She's fine, thank heavens," Alex said.

Smyth's thin lips all but disappeared off his face when he scowled and he was scowling now. "What were you thinking, taking her with you?" he growled.

Alex almost blurted out something like, "You think I'd leave her alone?" Only trouble was, the chief was right. He'd endangered her, not protected her. He should have hustled her out of that shed the moment he saw the broken window. Instead he said, "It seemed like a good idea at the time."

"Well, it wasn't. Furthermore, Kit Anderson reports the hasp on the door of the shed had been removed. I take it you're responsible for that, too?"

"I was just looking around," Alex said. Once again the image of Smyth standing close to that dwindling stack of index cards played in his mind.

"By breaking and entering?"

Alex didn't respond. He was angry and he wasn't sure he had a right to be.

Smyth jabbed the air between them. "I'm told you made a deposit in the evidence room last night."

"I found a drawer in that little table in the shed," Alex explained. "There were directions for how to fill a hypodermic needle with drugs and inject it into a plastic bottle so no one would know the contents had been tampered with. Maybe the lab can lift fingerprints or analyze the writing. It could help the government with their investigation."

"If you haven't jeopardized the provenance of that evidence," Smyth said sternly. "You should have handed it over to Kit."

"Since when do I hand evidence to Kit?" Alex asked.

"Since now."

There was a moment of silence, broken when Dylan cleared his throat. He looked at Smyth. "Where were you last night, Chief?"

"Not that it's any of your business, but I had a meeting," Smyth said as he rubbed his bald head.

Alex took a deep breath. "The shed is destroyed, right?"

"Totally," Smyth said.

"It's true I broke into it, but someone else did it first only they came in through the window. The place had been ransacked. The only thing I could see that was missing was the big model of the red-and-white biplane that used to hang over the table. The Cummings twins helped with the model and they were anxious to get it back, so someone should talk to them."

"We may be able to use that in further questioning," Smyth allowed. "I had them in yesterday for another round of interviews. I can't say they divulged anything new. Neither one of you mention this to anyone else, okay?"

"Okay," Alex said. "I should also mention the FBI reports the man known as William Tucker is actually Charles Bond. They have currently lost track of him."

"You spoke to the FBI?" Smyth snapped.

"Yeah."

"Did you mention what you found?"

"No, not yet. The agent was in a hurry and I thought you should be part of any exchange of that kind of information. I'm sure they'll be contacting you."

"Yes," Smyth interrupted. "I should think so." He nodded decisively. "I have another meeting this afternoon," he said, zeroing in on Alex. "We're busier than a mosquito at a nudist colony getting ready for God knows what disaster. I can't change any of that but by golly, I can change this. I want you to step back."

"What?" Alex said, stunned.

"Let Dylan and Kit handle this case. You're off it."

"But—"

"I think all that time in the mountains made you forget you're part of a team. And I'm in charge of this team, not you. Stop going off like some lone wolf looking for glory. And if I hear you're tampering with anything at all, there will be hell to pay. When I think what a reporter could lead with when it comes to this…well, it doesn't bear considering."

Alex blinked a couple of times. His mind raced to make sense of what he was hearing. What in the world was going on?

"I don't want to have to give you a reprimand or time off, but I will if I have to, no matter what happens to me."

Alex met the chief's gaze and did his best not to appear defiant or challenging since he figured that would just make things worse.

"I'll see you later," Smyth said to Dylan, then stalked back to his car and took off.

"What was that all about?" Dylan demanded.

Alex shook his head, bewildered. "I really don't know. Maybe he's got trouble at home or something."

"He's too pious to have trouble at home. Mr. Goody-two shoes is all about smoothing things over."

Alex had never heard Frank Smyth described

that way. "You sound like you know him pretty well. Do you know his wife, too?"

"Not really. They're both involved in a lot of civic and church activities. Word gets around."

And Dylan always seemed to have his ear close to the ground. "Well something is bothering the guy," Alex mused. "Maybe he feels bad Lynda died the way she did after he'd promised his mother he'd watch out for her. Is he handling her estate?"

"What estate?"

"You know, her house—"

"The chief owns everything," Dylan interrupted. "The land, the trailer, the whole nine yards. Lynda lived in it for twenty-some-odd years and there's no record of her paying a dime in rent."

"How do you know all this stuff?" Alex asked.

"It's a matter of record, buddy." Not to be deterred, Dylan continued. "Did you notice the equipment out there?"

"The tractor and Dumpster? Yeah. When did you see it?"

"I drove by this morning before I got here. Our trusty chief is getting ready to level that dump. He's had it declared a health hazard and rumor has it, he's hurrying things along to get it demolished. Makes you wonder what's he's hiding, doesn't it? And who is he meeting with that he won't name? Why so secretive?"

Alex wasn't a big fan of idle speculation, although he couldn't help but be interested. Was the chief involved in something dangerous? There was absolutely nothing to go on to suggest such a thing. So Smyth was acting surly—that didn't make him a criminal.

But why had he all of a sudden called Alex off this case?

"All I'm saying," Dylan said, "is that I'm keeping my eyes open. Be honest, what are you out here looking for?"

Glad to get off the topic of the chief, Alex resumed his systematic search of the terrain. "I'm wondering if Billy was hit on his way home from my house last Saturday night. It was crummy weather and we know his bike didn't get to the theater by itself. It's a long way to go in the fog."

"I'm sorry, but this seems like a fool's errand to me. If someone hit him out here, why move him to the theater and not the hospital?"

"The only reason I can surmise is they wanted an out-of-the-way place to finish him off. I'm pretty sure someone really didn't want him to talk to me."

"If you're right about Billy being involved with your crash, why in the world would he want to talk to you the minute you got back to town?"

"I'm not sure about that." Alex caught the glint of sunlight off of a piece of metal down in the gulch off the steep roadbed. He scrambled down the slope, Dylan on his heels. He slid a couple of feet on some shale and knelt to examine his find, a small piece of red plastic encased in chrome.

"This looks like part of a taillight housing off a bike," Alex said, and then his shoulders stiffened. The dirt around them had been disturbed with parallel tracks as though something, or someone, had been dragged up the gully. It wasn't visible from above. Rain had washed most of it away, but from down here, it was pretty obvious. A small, darker patch of earth off to the left under the cover of a bush made his stomach roll. A combination of intuition and experience kicked into gear.

He'd be willing to bet that dark patch of dirt had been saturated with blood. Billy's blood. Had the boy been hit, tumbled down the slope, laid here bleeding until someone dragged him back up the slope and drove him and his mangled bike away?

Beside him, Dylan groaned as though Alex had spoken all of this aloud. "I'd better get the techs to go back over the Cummings twins' car," he said, his voice subdued. He glanced at Alex and added, "You better let me handle this now. You heard what the chief said."

"I don't care what the chief said," Alex stated boldly. "I'm in the middle of this, which means my family is in the middle. I'm not backing off for anyone."

"But—"

Alex looked his partner in the eye. "Maybe it's because I'm going to be a father, I don't know. But this is about more than me. This is about our country and our freedom to make decisions. It's about our future. I know that sounds kind of over-the-top, but it's the way I feel. On a broad level, this is your fight as much as mine, I get that. But in my heart, this fight belongs to me."

Dylan nodded once, his gaze impenetrable. "Okay," he finally said. "If that's the way it is, that's the way it is."

"That's the way it is."

Chapter Twelve

As it was the Friday before a holiday, school let out an hour earlier than usual. Jessica had seen an ad about a sale on garden plants over near Campton, and with the sun shining and an extra hour of free time, she asked Silvia Greenspan to accompany her on the ride to the nursery.

"It's supposed to be sunny tomorrow and I want to be prepared," she explained.

"I just can't right now," the older woman said, holding up a stack of papers. "It's almost the end of the year and I have a ton of work."

"Don't worry about it," Jessica said. "It's only a half-hour drive and I'm restless again. It seems I can't sit still lately."

"I was like that when I was pregnant with my youngest," Silvia said.

Jessica headed out of town with a light heart until she drove by Billy's house and caught sight of the burned-out hulk in the backyard. The place looked depressing in the rain, the equipment waiting nearby like vultures hovering over a rotting corpse.

She looked away at once. Being pregnant demanded optimism and hope, it demanded faith in the future and a positive attitude and she was tired of being afraid.

Once at the garden center, she chose plants already established with set-on buds to hurry the bloom time. She mimicked the choices she'd chosen for her yard several weeks before when she gave Billy instructions. She started toward the checkout line, pushing a cart laden with pots of impending glory. It looked as though she and Alex would spend their Memorial Day vacation digging in the dirt.

If he got a vacation. With one confirmed murder and another death hanging over their heads as a possible homicide, to say nothing of a potential Memorial Day bloodbath, nothing was for sure.

As for why she still felt sentimental over the death of a young man who it appeared had gone out of his way to try to kill the man she loved—that was harder to pin down than the flowers. There was just some part of her brain that couldn't combine the image of Billy, the kid out in the garden, and Billy, the guy sneaking around Alex's airplane, doing his best to make sure Alex didn't have a chance of survival.

Maybe it *was* Tad and Ted who had organized all this. Maybe they used Billy. Maybe they were into drugs. Maybe, maybe, maybe.

Her phone rang and she smiled when she saw the call was from Alex. It was four o'clock and she couldn't wait to see him again. She answered it and the call immediately disconnected. She knew she had the mountains to thank for that, and she was glad she'd texted him her plans before taking off. At least he wouldn't worry about her.

Still, a gnawing pit opened up in her stomach and she debated returning the plants to their shelves and driving back into cell range. At that exact moment she felt the first fluttering kick of her baby and she touched her abdomen in awe.

This was the moment she'd been waiting for, and a rush of pleasure bathed her in what felt like sunlight. She smiled and her resolve strengthened. Life had to go on. There were these issues now, there'd be others later. In a way, the destruction of her garden had been like a metaphor for life—just keep going. Fix what's wrong, replace what's lost.

The clerk was an attractive blonde in her late forties. "You're going to be busy," she said as Jessica approached with a rolling cart covered with plants. "I hope you have a van or something."

"My car has a big trunk," Jessica said.

"You chose a nice variety," the clerk added, and she began scanning the bar codes.

"Someone destroyed our garden and we're starting over," Jessica explained. "Pity these won't be blooming in time for Memorial Day."

"Why?"

"Because I take flowers to the graves of veterans on Memorial Day, to honor my grandfather, you know?"

"Oh, my gosh," the woman said. "So do I. Red, white and blue?"

"If possible."

"But I live over in Blunt Falls," the clerk added.

"I do, too," Jessica laughed. "Hey, maybe I'll see you there."

"That'd be great," the clerk said.

"I go midmorning," Jessica added.

"I do, too," the clerk said, accepting Jessica's credit card. "Do you have a big yard?" Jessica explained what had happened to her flower garden. As she spoke, the clerk's eyes got wider and wider.

"That's terrible," she said. "It's so much work to create something beautiful and then to have it wantonly destroyed, makes you wonder what the world is coming to."

"Most people are good and decent," Jessica said with conviction. "Some aren't, but they're in the minority." *At least I hope they are,* she thought, embarrassed that she'd gotten so serious.

"Yeah, you're right, but I do have to say there are more than a few creeps lurking in the corners. Either that or I'm just a creep magnet. Well, is there anything else?"

"Nope. That should keep us busy."

ALEX WENT INTO the office the next morning to finish up paperwork he'd started earlier, before the chief got so adamant about him staying out of things. It was Saturday and with some shock he realized he'd been in this same office one week ago today making sure he still had a job. In a way, he was back in the same position.

But what he really wanted to be doing was helping Jessica plant her new garden. He'd unloaded the car for her the night before and while his plan had been to discuss the chief's confusing behavior with her, he'd backed away from the subject. She'd been in a great mood, happy and full of plans and chatter about a nice woman she met. She'd felt their baby kick for the first time and they spent an hour that night lying in bed with his hand on her abdomen waiting for him to experience it, as well. So far, no luck, but that would change.

"I didn't expect to find you sitting here smiling to yourself," Dylan said as he perched on the edge of Alex's desk.

"Just thinking," he said.

"About Jessica, no doubt."

"No doubt," Alex agreed. "Let me see your report."

"I don't think so," Dylan said.

"Why not?"

"Because you got warned off the case or have you forgotten?"

"I haven't forgotten."

Dylan stared at him a second, then shook his head. "Buddy, I'm going to be blunt. Before your crash you admitted to me you and Jessica were thinking of breaking up. Then you come back and discover she's pregnant. You can't walk away even if you want to."

"I don't want to," Alex said.

"Well, man, see, that's the thing. What about her? I mean, she was so sure you might have run out on her that she placed that remark on Facebook. You show up, what's she supposed to do but give it another shot? I know she wants to stop working for at least a year or two, you told me that. She needs your paycheck to make that happen. If you keep pushing, you could lose your job. Have you thought about what that might mean?"

"Are you implying she'd leave me?" Alex asked.

"I don't know," Dylan said as he glanced up. His expression changed. Alex looked to see what had caught his attention and found Smyth approaching.

"The bottom line is that it doesn't matter," Alex

said softly. "I have to keep digging. There is no option. I told you that."

Smyth paused at Alex's desk. "Digging for what?" he said, eyebrows furrowed, eyes glinting.

"Nothing," Alex said. "We're planting a new garden and that takes digging."

"The newspapers will eat that up."

"The newspapers could care less."

"I heard about what you found out on the road," Smyth continued. "What part of 'back off' didn't you get? You better go home before you jeopardize this whole investigation."

"Listen," Alex said, "I know I stretched the letter of the law the other night when I entered that shed…"

The chief shook his head. "You broke into private property and took evidence."

"That would have been destroyed if I hadn't taken it." He met Dylan's gaze because it was on the tip of his tongue to add that if the chief owned the place then what was the big deal? But Dylan seemed to know what Alex was thinking and his expression clearly said to tread softly.

"So help me, if those Cummings boys walk because you messed things up, Montana won't be big enough for the two of us," Smyth barked. "And by the way, just so you don't take me for a gullible fool, I know you weren't sick a few days ago, I know you dove on your plane, I even know you took a bottle of water out of the cockpit. That's probably another case you messed up, this one for the government. You're on quite a roll. I'm not going to reveal my sources so don't bother asking."

"Okay, I won't," Alex said.

"For both of you," the chief added, "the next two days are going to be busy with patrols at the parade and over at the fairgrounds where they've got some citywide rummage sale going. Lord almighty, why can't people just stay home? We're all pitching in for this. But for now, for today, Alex, you get out of here. I know how you like to dig in the dirt."

Dylan shook his head as the door closed behind Smyth. "I'm going to follow him."

"I don't think that's a good idea. He's acting strange. Did you tell him about the plane?"

"Not me," Dylan said. "Could it have been your friend?"

"You mean Nate?"

"No, the other guy. John Miter."

"I don't see how. I don't think he and the chief even know each other."

"I've seen them talking," Dylan said.

"When?"

"I can't remember. While you were missing. Just on the sidewalk or something." He pushed himself away from Alex's desk, which seemed to groan in relief and added, “I’ll call you when I discover what the chief is up to.”

Alex left soon after. He sat in his truck for a minute, unsure what to do. He kept thinking back to Billy.

The kid must have been drugged after he was hit, perhaps to keep him quiet while the perpetrator found a way to transport him to the drive-in. What had Lynda Summers really heard that night, and, if she was murdered, why?

His gut told him the Cummings boys didn’t have anything to do with Billy’s death. All sorts of people knew where their car was kept and that the key was left in the ignition.

Had the piece of Billy’s jacket found on the car gotten there when his bike was hit out on the road, or later, at the drive-in?

His phone rang and he saw by the number on the screen it was the lab. He was surprised the lab techs were working over the weekend, especially since it was a holiday weekend.

“What are you guys doing in?” he asked.

“I just came in because I knew you were anxious about this. We’ll finish testing on Tuesday. Meanwhile, the reflector you found came off Billy Summers’s bike. We’re going back over the Cummingses’ car. So far, no blood. In fact, dents and weeds notwithstanding, oh, and those pills, there’s nothing other than the fabric caught in the grill to tie it to Billy Summers."

"Judging from the roadside, he must have bled a lot," Alex said.

"It would seem so."

"How about the paint on Billy's bike?"

"Not a match. Same color, but different paint. There are a lot of red cars in the world, you know."

"Keep me posted," Alex said, wondering how long it would be before Smyth spread the word for them to do otherwise.

He drove around for a while, nervous about going home and letting Jessica see how uptight he was. He had to figure out a way to get a handle on things. It had started raining and the windshield wipers beat a monotonous thump-thump as they cleared the windshield. In some strange way, he was reminded of being in the Cessna, alone, high above the earth.

What had he overlooked? There must be something.

What did it mean that Frank Smyth owned Lynda Summers's land and home, and did it mean anything special that he was apparently ready to plow it under as soon as possible? The place was a dump; who could blame him for wanting to get rid of such a health hazard? Tuesday morning, Alex needed to check the property deed for himself.

Was the chief warning him off the case because

he was afraid Alex would find something that tied him to one or more deaths, maybe even to domestic terrorism?

And...how important was Alex's job? How much could he push without jeopardizing it? If he lost employment or went on unpaid leave, it would be impossible to find another job of the same caliber in Blunt Falls. They'd have to relocate.

He thought of what Dylan had said. Was Jess giving their marriage a chance solely because of his paycheck? There was no forgetting the way she'd acted when he first got home, as though she was undecided how she felt about him. He could remember the way she'd nervously folded clothes rather than sit next to him.

His phone rang again. This time he saw that it was Dylan calling and he realized he'd been driving aimlessly for over an hour. "Where are you?" he asked.

"Just saw the chief leave the bank with a briefcase that had to be full of money, what else?"

"Maybe he emptied his safe-deposit box," Alex said.

"Or maybe he made a big withdrawal. But why? Just wanted to let you know your trusty aide is on the job."

"Thanks," Alex said, and hung up. He'd pulled over for the call and now as he edged back into traffic, that old feeling of someone tracking him hit yet again. Searching his mirrors, he looked for anything out of place, but traffic looked pretty much like it always did midday Saturday and he could see nothing amiss.

What was he doing out here alone when Charles Bond could be driving into town, up to their front door? He made an abrupt turn and went home.

JESSICA SAT BACK on her heels and admired her handiwork. She doubted the garden would ever again look as it had under Billy's tender care, especially since there would soon be a child digging in the dirt and playing in a sandbox, but the promise of flowers in the months to come pleased her down to her soul.

It was a lonely weekend despite Alex's attempts to help her. When he was home, he was distracted and when he was at work, he just kind of disappeared. Since this was the weekend before the targeted Memorial Day, everyone at the station was pulling extra duty. Billy's murder had slipped to a back burner, on hold until after Monday, Alex explained, but there was something about the way he said it that made her wonder if he was being completely frank with her.

On Sunday, she picked up the flowers from the store and spent much of the day making small bouquets, tying them with red, white and blue ribbons and storing them in the refrigerator for delivery the next morning. Alex had said because he had parade duty later in the day, they would have to go very early so he could be with her. That was fine, she didn't care when they went, although the thought crossed her mind that she would miss seeing the nice clerk from the nursery.

Monday dawned overcast and nasty with promises of thunder and rain to come. "I guess it's a good thing we're going out to the cemetery first thing this morning," she told Alex.

"No kidding. I have to be at work by eleven, so we should leave right after breakfast."

They ate a quick meal and opened the closet for rain gear. She was zipping her slicker when Alex got a call and the look on his face as he took it made her cringe inside.

"Change of plans," he said after a few terse words. He grabbed his service pistol from the top shelf of the closet and slid it in the holster. "I have to go."

"Where? Who was that?"

"Dylan. He needs me right now."

"I'll go with you," she said.

"No. I'm sorry, but this is too dangerous. I'm not going to put you in jeopardy like I did with that bomb."

She pulled the coat closer around her body and held it. "You're scaring me," she said. "What does Dylan want?" As he stared at her, she all but stamped her foot. "Be honest, Alex. I know something is wrong."

"He's been following Chief Smyth."

"What? Why?"

Alex seemed to have to struggle to get the words out. "Because the chief's been acting odd. Toward me. Nasty, almost. Dylan swore to get to the bottom of it and now he says Smyth is out at the Summers place and he's not alone."

"Who's he with?" she insisted.

"Dylan says it's either Charles Bond or his double. I seriously doubt this is the case, but I do have to go. You wait here. I'll be back as soon as I can."

She nodded once, unwilling to send him off worried about her, but just as determined to go about her life. What was her option? Sit here alone and wait for news Alex had been shot? *No, thank you.* "Be careful," she said.

He kissed her. "I'm sorry I kept this to myself. I should have shared it with you."

She kissed him back and sent him on his way, but there was an old familiar ache in her heart.

ALEX DROVE AS fast as he dared. He couldn't wrap his head around Smyth and Bond meeting at Lynda's house of all places. The skies just kept growing more and more ominous and the weight of the clouds seemed to mirror the weight in his own heart.

He'd think about Jessica later. For now he made himself blot out the look of disappointment he'd seen in her eyes.

Twenty minutes later, he pulled up on the other side of the hedge outside the house. Dylan had pulled his car behind a dense copse of trees and was mostly out of sight. Alex was surprised his partner had chosen such a spot because of the inevitable scratches to the paint.

Alex moved quickly and silently toward the property, stepping over the yellow police tape that had been broken and now dangled down into the mud. Smyth's sedan was parked close to the double-wide. There were no other vehicles in sight, though the acrid smell of the fire still filled the air. The yard was muddy now where fire trucks had disturbed the soil a few nights before. Had whoever Smyth been meeting with already left?

"Psst..." Dylan said from a couple of feet away.

Alex hotfooted it to the bushes behind which Dylan stood. His partner was wrapped in a dark slicker, his face and hair wet, though the rain had just started to gently fall. "They're in the kitchen," he said.

"Maybe we could sneak around back—"

"No, I tried that. You can't hear anything. The front door is ajar. We'll have to chance going in."

"But there's only the one car," Alex said. "Did the meeting break up?"

"No. Smyth stopped at that motor lodge outside of town, this guy got in and they drove out here together."

Alex delayed. If Smyth caught him spying on him, he'd have a major fit. Worse, he'd probably fire him outright and he'd probably have just cause. Entering a building unlawfully, trespassing now.

"You're right to hold back," Dylan said suddenly. "Listen, you stay here. I'll go…"

"No," Alex said, his mind snapping back into focus. He pulled out his cell and put it on Vibrate, shoved it back in his pocket. This was about way more than Billy's murder or Lynda Summers's death. If Frank Smyth was involved with the militant terrorists responsible for killing Mike and all the others, responsible for putting a bullet hole in Nate and terrorizing Jessica, then this was Alex's fight. Job or no job, future or no future.

"Cover me," he said as he pulled his pistol. He crept up the steps and across the threshold, Dylan right behind him.

The house greeted him as it always did, with boxes still wobbling on top of one another, bags of junk still overflowing. If anything it appeared more squalid than ever and it certainly smelled worse as years of garbage continued to rot in the corners. He breathed through his mouth so he wouldn't gag, then turned and met Dylan's gaze.

He signaled for Dylan to stay put and tiptoed toward the kitchen, sliding on a pile of overturned magazines, catching himself by grabbing the wall. He stood without breathing for a moment, sure he must have been heard, but there was still no sound coming from the kitchen. He continued forward, deeper into the house, where the light had trouble penetrating and the smell got worse and worse.

The kitchen was new territory to him, but here, too, movement was restricted by rubbish. It appeared there might have once been stacks, but now things were overturned, upended as though they'd fallen or been pushed aside during a fight. Two open bottles of beer, both half-drunk, occupied the only clear drain-board space and from the beads of moisture on the glass, it was obvious they were fresh.

Where were the two men? Had they battled their way out to the backyard? He could see a corner of the door and it appeared closed.

The place smelled like hell. If that wasn't the stench of fresh blood, he didn't know what was and it raised the hairs on the back of his neck. He rounded the counter to a relatively clear spot and stopped dead in his tracks.

Frank Smyth lay in a pool of his own congealing blood, which had also sprayed and splattered everything around him. The poor guy looked like he'd been through a meat grinder. There was no way he could have survived, and even as Alex knelt to feel for a pulse he knew there could be none. An unopened briefcase lay close by.

So, Smyth had met with Bond. They must have been in it together. Bond must have decided to cut his losses and get rid of Frank. Maybe they'd been using this house as a meeting spot. Maybe Lynda had gotten in the way.

All these thoughts bombarded his head in the time it took to get back to his feet and turn around. Dylan stood behind him, his weapon drawn, as well. He lowered his arm as his gaze darted past Alex. "Oh, my God," he said, pointing to a corner. "What's that?"

Alex looked around the room again and there by the door he saw something that sent a chill down his spine.

A machete lay on the floor. A machete with a dark green cord knotted around the handle. His machete. The blade was covered with fresh blood. He walked over to the discarded weapon and leaned down again to make sure. It was his, all right. His initials were written in indelible ink on the shaft.

He felt a cold round pressure against the back of his head. "Put down your gun and stand up. And so help me, if you try anything I will make sure Jessica faces a worse fate than the chief."

Dylan's voice. Dylan.

"What the hell are you doing?" Alex said, but he knew. No wonder Dylan was wet and covered with a raincoat. He must have been covered in the chief's blood and washed it off before calling.

"Put the gun down," Dylan repeated, and emphasized his remark with a jab to Alex's head.

Alex set the gun down on the floor and stood. Dylan kicked it aside where it spun out of Alex's reach.

"Did you do this to Frank?" Alex demanded. "Why?"

"Oh, Alex, don't be so dense. Who do you think is Charles Bond's Blunt Falls accomplice? Come on, dude."

"Are you behind everything?" Alex said, trying to merge his partner, Dylan Hobart, with this lunatic.

Dylan nodded. "All the little mishaps and innuendos, Jess's race to the emergency room, the garden, a couple of deaths…this and that, yeah, that's all me."

"Are you trying to tell me you got Frank Smyth to drink a beer with you, then lay down on the floor so you could hack him to death?"

"Frank was coming here with a briefcase filled with money because someone threatened to tell everyone he was Billy Summers's father." Dylan grinned. "You didn't know that about our chief, did you? It's true. He and Lynda had a thing for a while. I guess it was before he found religion. Hell, maybe it's *why* he found religion. He got Lynda pregnant about a month after he knocked up his wife. God forbid his precious daughter ever find out."

"How can you possibly know this?" Alex said.

Dylan smiled. "Lynda may have let herself and her house go, but she was still good for a hot time on that couch of hers. Frank did me a favor when he kept sending me over here to calm her down. Sometimes she indulged in a little postcoital chatter. Amazing what a sex-drunk woman will tell you."

"I don't believe it," Alex said.

"I like them older. Young hotties are for show-and-tell. Anyway, I pretended I'd shown up to meet you here, too, got Frank to unwind a little by drinking a drugged beer and then used your machete to whack him. He didn't put up much of a fight and everyone knows you've been a little high-strung since you got back. Frank even talked to the mayor about suspending you. I guess you got wind of it and decided to take him out."

Alex tried to wrap his head around the craziness. "Why would Frank want to suspend me?"

"Because he is, or rather, *was,* under the impression you vandalized your own yard and then made sure you kept yourself the center of attention. He also thought you were hiding evidence like this machete. He was beginning to think you might even have killed Billy Summers yourself. He's a gullible man, no matter what he said. He'll believe anything you tell him if you tell him in the right way."

"Then it was you who set Billy up to sabotage my plane," Alex stated matter-of-factly.

"It wasn't hard. I made it sound like a prank and I gave him a little money so he could work on his models. And then the little jerk found a conscience and started following Jessica around like a lost puppy. By the time you got home, he couldn't wait to spill his guts and confess."

"Which you couldn't let happen."

"Not so much. I ran him down after your party. He was cut up pretty bad but he wasn't dead. I had a few of those Rohypnol pills we took off that loser last year in the car. Two little forget-everything pills threw Billy for a loop. I'd seen a tarp out at the Summers place, so I drove there to get it. Didn't want my car to get too dirty. I think Lynda saw me. She kind of hinted she did and I knew sooner or later, she'd get chatty with someone else. I knew I'd have to get rid of her soon so I did. Anyway, when I got back, Billy was trying to claw his way up the hill. I knocked him out, dragged him and his bike up the hill, wrapped him up in the tarp and stuck him in the trunk. His bike went in the backseat." He paused for a second and shook his head. "It was a tight fit. And then I thought of the drive-in theater."

"Billy was never in the Cummingses' car," Alex said. "You planted the evidence when you went out to question them and then you started rumors. That's why there's no blood on their car. And your girlfriend wasn't rear-ended in Billings. You needed an out-of-town body shop because the front was damaged when you hit Billy."

"Aren't you the clever one? They brought it back to me the day you flew up to the lake. Great timing."

Alex shook his head. "You're part of these domestic terror groups? You, Dylan? I had no idea you held such deeply seated beliefs." As he spoke, his phone vibrated with a text. It might as well have vibrated on the moon.

Dylan barked a laugh. "I'm not some crazy crackpot like Bond and the others," he said. "What they do is certifiable. If people are stupid enough to cave to their tactics, so be it. I participate solely because of the money, plain and simple. New cars, steroids, pumping iron, sex, excitement, it's all the same. You were supposed to disappear forever, that was the plan. A Boy Scout like you is problematic for an entrepreneur like me. I was delighted when that loony in Shatterhorn paid me to screw with your plane."

Alex's mind was still playing catch up as past

events demanded examination under this bright new light of discovery. "You weren't on a date Thursday night," he said. "You were here breaking into the shed. Why'd you take the biplane?"

Dylan shrugged. "I'm toying around with hooking it back to the Cummings boys. 'Keep your options open,' that's my motto."

"Then you watched Jess and me discover the drawer in the table that you missed. You wrote the directions for Billy, your prints might have been on that card. You threw the Molotov cocktail to get rid of the evidence."

"To get rid of the evidence and to get rid of you," Dylan stated, his eyes hard, the bantering tone now absent. He lowered the aim of his gun to Alex's knee. It was the one hurt in the crash and it suddenly throbbed like hell. The gun barrel inched up to aim at his groin next with similar results. "Now, with Frank dead and you about to die by a bullet from his gun, I can spin things any way I want."

A layer of sweat broke out on Alex's brow. How could he have known and worked with this man for three years and never seen the cold-blooded egotism behind his eyes? "Forensics will be all over this," he said. "There are no powder burns on Smyth's hand—"

"Won't matter," Dylan said, pulling a cigarette lighter from his pocket. Alex recognized it as belonging to the chief and he knew the man's initials were engraved in the metal casing. "You know, any other guy would have said, 'Screw this, I'm taking my wife and moving away from here,' but not you. So I put a bug in Frank's ear. He got the impression you were messing with this case so he'd look bad and you could have his job.

"Then he started getting blackmail letters and you got credit for those, too. I gave him the same drug I gave Billy, the rest of which they'll find in your pocket. Well, if there's anything left of you, that is." He held the flame next to a pile of newspapers that immediately began to burn.

"Dylan, think about what you're doing. Not just to me but to the country."

"I'll be the new chief by tomorrow," Dylan said calmly as he threw the lighter across the room. "I'll get rid of the index cards and explain you and Smyth away." He picked up the briefcase. "So long, buddy. All your high-flying ideals are for nothing. It's too late. You can't stop what's going to happen. You should have stayed in the mountains."

The deadly sound of gunfire cracked the air. Alex gasped before he realized he hadn't been hit. Instead, Dylan crumpled to the floor with an unholy scream and a splatter of blood. Alex immediately slid himself across the room to grab his own weapon, exploding to his feet, ready to fire.

And met the steely-eyed gaze of John Miter, armed to the teeth. He stood over Dylan's prone, writhing body, an impassive expression on his face. Blood covered Dylan's now empty gun hand and his wounded thigh. Invectives and empty threats spewed from his mouth.

"The fire is spreading," John said matter-of-factly.

Alex glanced over his shoulder. In the midst of the adrenaline-charged past few seconds, he'd all but forgotten about the flames; now the crackling, smoky blaze was already too big for them to extinguish without help. They both grabbed one of Dylan's arms and hauled him upright. John snatched the briefcase and the three of them stumbled their way out of the burning double-wide.

"What are you doing here?" Alex asked John as they erupted into the fresh air.

"I've been watching your back ever since we tested your Vita-Drink," he said. "Nate kind of asked me to keep an eye on you."

"You're the one who's been following me."

"When I can. You shouldn't have known I was there, though. I must be losing my edge."

Alex slapped his shoulder. "I never saw you," he assured him. Dylan had slumped onto the wet grass and now Alex leaned over him, catching his collar in one hand. "What did you mean it's too late?"

Dylan smirked through gritted teeth.

"Is Jessica in danger?" Alex demanded, grabbing Dylan by the collar.

Dylan groaned. "Jessica. She's all you ever think of. No, you moron, Charles Bond is here. What's going to happen is bigger than your precious little wife."

"How do you know Charles Bond?" Alex demanded.

"We go way back," Dylan said, some of the bravado resurfacing. "Back to before New Orleans. We lifted weights at the same gym but he was an old guy, at least to me. I thought he was killed in the explosion just like everyone else did. Could have knocked me over with a feather when he called here a few months ago."

"Was he behind the bombing that supposedly killed him?"

"No way. It was just a lucky break as far as he was concerned. Gave him a nice, clean start. Then he fell in with his brother-in-law in Shatterhorn and climbed aboard the crazy zealot bus. He tried to coax me into helping him by talking about ideals. When he finally started changing the language to money, well, that's when I started listening."

"Is he going after the parade?" Alex said, just about ready to smash Dylan's nose into his face.

Grimacing, Dylan waited a second, then nodded.

"You go, I'll stay with him," Miter said as the

fire inside the trailer blew a window. "I'd appreciate you telling your buddies not to shoot me when they get here."

Alex dropped Dylan and ran to his truck. He raced downtown with his heart in his throat while placing call after call. First the fire department, then the mayor's office and Carla Herrera. Kit Anderson was in charge of the officers patrolling the parade that would start in less than two hours, so his call came next. Then Agent Struthers who promised to beef up federal law-enforcement involvement.

The only one Alex couldn't reach was Jess.

Chapter Thirteen

The cemetery was surprisingly well visited in spite of the drippy skies, explained, in part, because of preparations underway for a graveside ceremony at the top of the hill. Workmen had raised an awning over a freshly dug grave. An elderly woman in a long, dark coat stood watching them, head bowed, gloved hands resting atop a cane, framed by a nearby crypt and the dark silhouette of trees.

Jessica easily found her grandfather's grave situated close to an old grove of oaks. "Here you go, Grandpa," she said, setting the first bouquet of the day in his flower holder. She paused, as was her habit, to draw on memories of him, but her thoughts immediately darted to Alex, and she took out her phone to text him. She wasn't surprised when he didn't respond and crossed her fingers that he was safe.

"Hi," a woman said, and Jessica looked up to see a blonde in a black raincoat walking toward her. She carried a basket of small bouquets much like the one Jessica held as well as an umbrella.

Jessica recognized her from the nursery. In a way she was glad to see her; in a way she was too distracted to even think about making small talk with a near stranger.

"Are you okay?" the woman asked.

Jessica nodded.

The woman touched her arm. "My name is Nancy," she said. "Is there anything I can do for you?"

"No, I'm fine," Jessica said as her attention was drawn to the sight of a hearse driving through the cemetery. A long line of cars with dimmed headlights followed behind. "My husband is…working," she explained as she watched the procession, which was hard not to view as ominous. "I…I miss him."

Nancy nodded with understanding, her gaze following Jessica's. "That's one of the reasons I'm here," she said, nodding toward the hearse. "The service on the hill is for an army nurse who died last week. There was a big write-up in the newspaper about her. She's credited with saving the lives of two dozen orphans during the Korean Conflict."

"I didn't see the article," Jessica said, glimpsing the older woman in the black coat slowly walking away from the new grave. She still leaned heavily on her cane as though the weight of the world had settled on her thin shoulders. "I haven't read the paper lately."

"I read about her last night and thought I'd pay my respects," Nancy said. "Want to join me?"

Jessica started to refuse, then changed her mind. Nancy seemed to be easy company and she didn't want to be alone. "Thanks, I'd like that. By the way, I'm Jessica Foster."

Nancy's brow furrowed. "That name sounds familiar."

"Well, I did charge all those plants."

"No, it's not that. Wait, is your husband a cop?"

"Yes. Do you know him?"

"No, not really. I just met him a few days ago. He was with a walking muscle named Dylan."

Jessica nodded. "They're partners."

"Are they close?"

"I suppose."

Nancy nodded, giving Jessica the distinct feeling she was holding something back.

"Let's walk on up the hill," Jessica said, curious now.

As they approached the awning and the growing crowd, the older woman in the long coat had almost reached the crypt. As she slowly turned and surveyed the gathering she'd just left, her gaze met Jessica's. Jessica sucked in her breath and looked away.

"What's wrong?" Nancy said as she opened her umbrella to ward off the increasing rain.

"Nothing," Jessica said, darting a glance over her shoulder.

The old woman stood in front of the crypt, seemingly oblivious to the weather, lost in thought.

BY THE TIME Alex arrived downtown, traffic was already plugged. He parked in a loading zone and ran along the sidewalk to the fountain outside the courthouse where he'd arranged over the phone to meet Kit Anderson. Kit's usual air of superiority had been shaken in the wake of learning what had happened to the chief and that the man no one wanted to ever come to Blunt Falls was allegedly already here.

"I called Campton," Alex said by way of greeting. "They're sending over all their off-duty police to help."

"The sheriff's department responded, too," Kit said. "I think there'll be more police here than spectators, especially if this rain gets any heavier." He shook his head. "I still can't believe Dylan killed the chief."

"Among other things," Alex said as his phone rang. It was John. As he answered it, he remembered the text that had come back when Dylan held the upper hand and things looked really bad. He'd check his messages after this call.

"Your buddy started to laugh after you left," John Miter said.

"Why?"

"That's what I wondered. He didn't want to explain what was so funny until I accidentally stepped on his shot-up hand. I can be so clumsy."

"Who the hell are you, really?" Alex said. "Tell me the truth."

"I'm John Miter, an old retired guy who likes to fish."

"You know what I mean, John."

There was a slight pause and his voice dropped. "Let's just say I know my way around people like this. Anyway, what I wanted to tell you is that I don't think anything is going to happen at that parade."

"Because?"

"Because Dylan finally choked out that you were going to the wrong place."

"Do you believe him?"

"I don't know for sure, Alex, but there was another nasty laugh like he'd put one over on you and then the ambulance arrived, so he clammed up. Are there any other events planned for the day?"

"There's a citywide rummage sale at the fairgrounds. I'd better get more people out there, too."

"Or here's another thought. What if this Bond guy isn't coming here at all? What if Dylan is still yanking your chain?"

"And what if he's not?"

"Okay, I see your point. Good luck," he said and disconnected before Alex could belatedly thank him for saving his life. He checked his messages immediately and saw that Jess had tried to contact him. The first text told him she was at the cemetery, that she loved him and hoped he was okay. The second one said that she'd run across an important graveside service for a former army nurse and she was going to attend. She'd contact him afterward.

The cemetery.

A former soldier, a hero, laid to rest.

The Shatterhorn Killer had never killed in volume. It was the unexpected terror and the erosion of confidence and hope he was after. Alex began running. Thunder crashed the sky. A bolt of lightning followed soon after. Maybe the parade would be called off. If so, that would send more people to the indoor rummage sale. He called Kit and told him to make sure to think of that should the parade fizzle out. He said he'd be gone for a few minutes but refused to provide an explanation.

His intuition was in high gear now and there was no turning back. It was a long shot, way too remote a possibility to call people away from the more obvious choices, but there was no way in the world he could keep himself from making sure.

His phone rang as he drove the truck out onto

the highway. The cemetery wasn't far and all the traffic was going in the other direction so he knew he'd make good time, but he also knew Jess's second text had come fifteen minutes earlier—how had he missed that? And why wasn't she answering now?

He answered without looking at the screen. "Foster here."

"Alex?"

"Jessica," he said with such profound relief that it knocked his breath away for a second.

"Where are you? Are you okay?"

"Didn't you get my text? Never mind. I'm at the cemetery. Listen, I have to tell you something about Dylan. I met this woman—"

"You don't have to tell me about him," Alex said.

"Yes, I do."

"I already know about him. This is important. Are you at the graveside service you mentioned?"

"I'm standing apart so I don't bother anyone with this call."

"I'm at the gate right now. Where is it being held?"

"At the top of the hill. Why are you here? I don't understand. What about Charles Bond? Did you see him?"

"Listen to me carefully. I've got this gut instinct

that Bond may target that funeral. Please, just trust me. Have you seen anything or anyone unusual?"

She paused for a second. "Not really. I'm looking around now. There's a crowd of people here under a sea of umbrellas. Mary Rivers's pastor is speaking about her years of service. The thunder stopped but it's raining like crazy and we're all getting soaked so I imagine they'll cut this short. Wait, I don't see the old woman. She must have left."

"What old woman?"

"There's a tall elderly lady here wearing a long black coat. She was near a big crypt a few minutes ago. Oh, wait, okay, I see her. She's walking toward the ceremony. Man, she's moving fast."

Alex frowned. "Why did this lady catch your attention?"

"It was just that her eyes… Well, I mean, when I looked at her earlier, it was like she looked right through me, like I was invisible. And her eyes were so dark and bright, they were kind of possessed. And now she's moving three times as fast and not using her cane—"

"Are you sure it's a woman?" Alex said, pulling the truck to a stop down the hill. He immediately jumped out. He could see the gathering up the slope but it was raining too hard to make out details. He quickly darted between gravestones, charging his way up the hill.

Jessica's voice wavered. "Of course. And yet, I don't know." A slight pause, and then a gasp. "That's not a cane."

"Listen to me, baby," he said urgently. "Get down low right now, down as close to the ground as you can. I'm on my way." And then he suddenly heard shots in stereo, both over his phone and from up the hill. Jess screamed once and fell silent. He stuffed the phone in his pocket as he pulled his weapon. He heard the sickening thud of more shots as he dashed up the slope as if his feet were on fire.

He erupted on the top by the crypt. Everyone in attendance had either started running or had hit the ground. What appeared to be an old woman stood over them, an assault rifle in her hands, her back to Alex. He silently moved toward her until he was only six feet away. All of a sudden, her gunfire ceased.

"Bond!" Alex yelled.

The old woman turned and came into focus as Charles Bond in disguise. He'd popped out an empty clip and as he stared at Alex, he jammed in another.

"It's over," Alex said. "I know about your brush with terrorism. This isn't making anything better."

Bond didn't respond.

"Put the weapon down."

Bond reached forward to charge the rifle.

Time was up. Alex fired.

Bond immediately fell to his knees and then twisted and landed on his back, faceup. Alex approached cautiously, his pistol pointed at his target.

The killing shot had hit Bond in the forehead, knocking the wig askew, revealing a bald head underneath. Even in death, Bond's eyes burned as the rain washed blood over his face. After taking the rifle, Alex was happy to turn away.

But what met his gaze was sobering. Those who hadn't run or hidden behind tombstones lay on the ground, their dark clothes and the pounding rain making bloodstains hard to see. People who hadn't been hurt were beginning to tend to those who had. Groans and whimpers increased. While he walked among everyone, he looked for Jessica but couldn't find her. He took out his phone and placed an emergency call. He didn't want to stop the police efforts underway at the rummage sale or the parade on the off chance there was another attack but they needed ambulances out here at once.

When he hung up, he did a one-eighty and that's when he finally saw Jess. She was kneeling over a woman, and he veered off in her direction. The victim looked vaguely familiar. Jess held her scarf against the woman's throat. He kneeled down next to his wife and she looked up at him, tears in her eyes.

"I got to her as fast as I could. Is she—" she began, her lips trembling.

He checked the woman's wrist. "No, she's not dead. Her heartbeat is strong. Keep applying pressure with that scarf. You're doing fine." He snatched an open umbrella lying on the ground nearby and held it over both women. The welcome sound of sirens reached them and their gazes met. "Are you okay?" he whispered.

"I think so. That old lady was really Charles Bond, wasn't it?"

"Yes," he said.

They both looked around the cemetery as people came to the aid of those who'd been wounded. Ambulances arrived, and finally a team of medics came to relieve Jessica of her task and transport the woman to the hospital. Alex sent the umbrella with them.

As they wheeled her away Jessica turned to him. She was wet and pale, tears mixing with raindrops, relief and sadness at war in her eyes. His heart melted at the sight of her. He'd thought he'd lost her. He ached to hold her and yet he was oddly frozen, waiting for something he couldn't name.

"I'm sorry I got annoyed you weren't sharing things with me," she mumbled. "I was afraid things were slipping back to how they had been. But that's not going to happen."

"No, it's not. Never again," he said. "I was

struggling with Smyth. Dylan had been playing us against each other. It was confusing and I retreated into myself. But it wasn't like the old days. I swear, it wasn't. I just needed time. And as it turns out, time was the one thing we didn't have a lot of."

"No marriage is perfect," she said softly, wiping rain out of her eyes with her fingers. "No relationship comes without struggles and compromises," she continued, gripping his hands. "The bottom line is that we love each other and we want to spend our lives together. Right?"

He pulled her tight against him. Their lips met and for him, at least, the sun burst through the clouds.

"Take me home," she said against his neck.

ALEX HAD TO go back to work, of course, as the mayor had appointed him temporary chief of police and there were a million loose ends to iron out. He'd told her about what happened out at Billy's old house during the drive home, and she was still shocked by all of it.

She'd watched the evening news and knew an attack at a Seattle food-and-wine festival had been averted. Maybe it was finally over—for now, anyway.

It surprised her when Alex walked in the door at seven that night. He looked ragged and worn but his smile warmed her. "I didn't expect you so early," she said, patting the seat next to her on the sofa.

"It will all still be there tomorrow," Alex said, yawning into his hand. "I'm done with it for tonight."

She took his hand and pulled him down to sit beside her. "Was there any more trouble in town?"

"No, thank goodness. The parade was canceled, the rummage sale went without a hitch. It was just the cemetery. Unfortunately, four people were injured. It's incredible the casualty toll wasn't higher. Makes me wonder if this wasn't Bond's swan song."

"What do you mean?"

"I wonder if he was tired of the scheme he was playing out. People were getting wise to his tactics, the fear angle had turned into anger. There was no hope he could influence people the way he wanted. I know these domestic militia terrorists groups are informally linked, if at all, but I think maybe in Bond's case he wanted out and this is how he chose to do it. Most of his bullets seemed to fly high and wide."

Jessica shivered.

"How is your friend?" he asked.

"She's going to be okay. They admitted her to the hospital and I went to see if she needed anything. Her parents had arrived by then." She looked closely at Alex and added, "She lives really close to Billy Summers. Did you know that?"

"I thought I recognized her. She's the gal with the great garden."

"Her name is Nancy Dill. She's also the person who told me about Dylan. That was before you told me everything else about Dylan."

"What did she say?"

"She told me that Thursday afternoon, Dylan came back to her house after you two had left."

"Must have been when I asked him to question neighbors he claimed weren't home. Damn, no wonder he didn't know one of the houses was abandoned."

"She said he was polite and charming. She told him to come back later for a beer. When he came back he was different. Full of himself, bragging about all his exploits, grabbing at her and making it clear what he wanted. She slapped him and told him to leave and he did. But she saw him pull off to the side of her driveway and run into the trees. That kind of made her nervous so she grabbed her keys and drove into Campton to spend the night with friends. She didn't know about the bomb or the fire."

Jessica studied Alex's strong profile. "When I heard her story, I realized he might have run through the woods and broken into Billy's shed. The timing was right. And that suggested he was the one who threw the Molotov cocktail. That's when I called you."

He nuzzled her hair. "I've never been so glad to hear anyone's voice before in my whole life." He pulled her to rest against his chest, his arms around her, his face close to her ear, his breath warm and comforting against her skin. "The last ten days make the time stranded in the mountains seem peaceful and soul affirming by comparison. How about we fly up there when the baby is old enough and camp on the lake?"

"I'd love that," she said. "Would you introduce me to the people who rescued you?"

"You bet."

"Nate called while you were gone," she added. "I told him what had happened. He and Sarah are flying back up here this weekend. He wants to hear all the details."

"That's great news," Alex said, sighing deeply.

"Alex, I can't believe John Miter saved your life. Who is he really?"

"I asked him. He wouldn't tell me."

"I guess we'll never know."

"As a matter of fact, I asked Agent Struthers about him. Once he stopped chortling, he swore me to secrecy except to you. John Miter is ex-CIA. He was a cold-war agent."

She looked up over her shoulder at him. "He was a spy? A real spy?"

Smiling, Alex nodded. "Apparently a damn good one, too."

"Let's have a little dinner party when Nate and Sarah get here. We'll invite John," she said as she positioned Alex's hands on her abdomen. "Maybe Silvia would like to come, too. Don't you think they'd make a good pair?"

He laughed. "A high-school principal and a retired spy. Why not?"

"Junior is having a frisky evening," she added with a murmur. "Maybe you can feel something."

They sat still for quite a while. To Jessica, the baby's antics were pronounced but when Alex failed to comment, she began to suspect he'd fallen asleep. Checking to see if she was right, she found herself looking at his face the moment the baby let loose with a big rolling kick. His lips curved and his eyes crinkled. "I bet you a dollar there's more than one in there," he said before kissing her forehead.

She nuzzled her face against his neck. "You're on."

* * * * *